KING OF
FOREVER

H. L. Macfarlane

COPYRIGHT

For every endless night when sleep escapes us.

It's only forever...not long at all.
Underground (D. Bowie; 1986)

PRØLØGUE

EVERY UNSEELIE WORTH THEIR SALT KNEW what was going on. Even the ghoul who had once been called Beira, currently enjoying a luxurious exile in the depths of Loch Lomond, was well aware of the rumblings of trouble between the faerie factions.

Beira's exile had not been quite so lovely back when she'd had to beware of the kelpie. The beast could have easily rent her flesh from her bones if he'd felt that way inclined; Beira had been very careful to sneak around and only risk drowning and devouring her next meal when she was quite certain he was miles away.

One hundred years ago she might have been a match for the kelpie. An intimidating witch by anyone's standards, with particular talents for prophecy and blood magic, in her quest for power and glory Beira had broken most every taboo known to faerie-kind. The Seelie Court had been the first of the factions to cast her out, though eventually even the far more vicious and bloodthirsty Unseelie – her own kin – banished her, too.

And so it was that Beira spent decades skulking from place to place, stripped of most of her power and influence, until she came upon Loch Lomond. It was dangerously close to the centre of the Seelie Court but, because of the even more dangerous kelpie, Beira knew she would face no problems from the faeries so long as she stayed within the confines of the water.

Beira knew the danger was worth the risk, anyway, for she wanted to be close to the Court in order to keep up-to-date with the ebb and flow of the faerie realm. It was imperative she was immediately informed when an opportunity finally arose for her to break her exile and regain her true and rightful power.

When she discovered that the kelpie was seeking her out Beira had been certain her end was nigh. But then the creature asked for her help. *Her* help. Beira, the all-powerful. Beira, the all-seeing. Beira, the bloodthirsty.

Though the first part was no longer true, no amount of binding faerie magic would ever strip Beira of her prophetic abilities. And she was just as bloodthirsty as she'd ever been; if she could strike up a deal with the kelpie wherein he left her to do as she pleased within his domain then she would gladly help him.

That the kelpie needed transformation magic had been a relief for it was the very limit of Beira's already limited abilities. He used his twelve hours in the form of a man well, going by the fact he had since regained his bridle. And, true to his word, the beast had largely left Beira alone since then.

On occasion he actively sought her out to join him in a hunt. But the kelpie spoke but rarely during these times and, when the hunt was over, would disappear for months on end. In reality he was hardly in the loch at all any more, choosing instead to live as a human with the Darrow girl who looked after the land.

"The Darrow girl, the Darrow girl," Beira sang in her twisted, ugly voice, though it had once been frightening and beautiful. She scanned the loch with wide, keen eyes, hunting down a human who had fallen beneath the surface. Their fear hung in the water, tantalisingly close by. She continued singing as she swam, the same line over and over again: "The Darrow girl will cause problems for you all."

In truth the Darrow girl had caused many problems *already* for both the kelpie and the golden King of the Seelie Court, but the biggest problems of all were yet to come to pass. It was true that the mortal would also bring great joy to those who loved her across the span of her life, but that joy came at a heavy price.

Beira wondered if that price would – or could – be paid.

"The silver king will come for you, girl," she murmured, eyes flashing in the dark water as she finally caught sight of the unfortunate soul who had fallen into the loch. A young boy, already drowned and sinking down, down, down. Beira wasted no time in darting out to claim him before any other wicked creature could. She placed a gentle kiss upon the boy's forehead as a gesture to his mother, who would despair to discover him lost.

Then she opened her maw wide around his skull and shattered it with one terrifying bite.

"The silver king is coming," Beira sang, long after all that remained of the boy were a few finger bones and the rags of his tattered clothes. "He is coming, and you have all run out of time."

CHAPTER ONE

Lachlan

It was raining, and Lachlan hated it. Under ordinary circumstances he would have deigned not to go outside, but today was different.

The last five years had passed like five minutes, and two months ago Lachlan celebrated his one hundred and fourth birthday. Now that he had lived a full century he could finally stand tall and true beside the older members of the Seelie Court, though by his kind's standards he was still very young indeed.

Especially to be king, as they keep reminding me, he thought dolefully. With the threat of war with the Unseelie simmering beneath the surface of every choice the Court made Lachlan had been subject to ever more criticism from his kin. He had been foolish to face up to Eirian with no way of winning against him, they said. They were right, of course, especially since the Unseelie king now had the worst kind of leverage against him.

That leverage was Sorcha Darrow.

But Lachlan could not find it in him to regret his feelings for the mortal woman, who was the reason he was standing outside in the rain, nor the hold she had over his heart. He loved her dearly, and deeply, in a way he might never admit aloud to anyone. His feelings for her cast a shadow over the love he held for his queen, Ailith, making it feel shallow and adolescent.

Though that may be because of her new consort. Lachlan pushed the thought away.

"Sometimes the mortals really do know how to put on a good funeral service."

Lachlan smothered a flinch of surprise at the voice, which belonged to his adviser, Ronan. The faerie was broad and burly, with curling horns like a ram's upon his head, though at present he was under the glamour of a human. Lachlan was, too, as were the rest of the faeries with him. For they were indeed at a mortal funeral: that of William Darrow.

Sorcha, whose usually wild hair was pinned back and impeccably tidy for once, stood by the edge of her father's grave with her bereft mother and her kelpie lover, Murdoch, by her side. A fine mist of winter drizzle enshrouded them all, causing their silhouettes to waver as if they, too, were made of water. When Margaret Darrow began to weep Murdoch swept her into his arms so that her tears could remain hidden from the rest of the funeral-goers.

Though it frustrated him that the kelpie had integrated himself into Sorcha's family in a way Lachlan could not, he kept his insecurities from showing on his face. He was not the kind of fool to interrupt the family during such a moment, after all, though Lachlan wanted nothing more than to console the woman he loved. No, he remained a polite distance away with his small cohort of faeries who wished to pay their last respects to the kind and loving human that was William Darrow.

The man had been keeper of the land around both the loch and the forest his entire life, protecting everyone from all manner of threats from greedy, selfish mortals. In his later years he had passed that duty onto his daughter due to his ailing health, thus keeping the Darrow tradition alive. The faeries owed a great deal to the family, though they knew humans in general were becoming a bigger and bigger threat against their supernatural way of life.

Sorcha and the kelpie's battle against Murdoch Buchanan's old work colleagues was chilling proof of that.

The beast wearing Murdoch's skin cast his eyes over to Lachlan. A curt nod passed between them, then the man who was not a man returned his attention to Sorcha and her mother. Lachlan reached a hand out across the graveyard towards Sorcha, thinking that perhaps it wouldn't hurt to say a few words to her, but Ronan gently touched his wrist to stop him.

"Leave her for now, Lachlan," he said, not unkindly. "Miss Darrow and the kelpie are coming to the Court this evening, are they not? Save your words and sympathies for then."

Yet Lachlan could not help but take a step or two towards Sorcha until his keen ears could pick up on the muffled sobs of Margaret Darrow through the rain as she cried against Murdoch's chest.

"He would have l-loved to see you two m-married," she wailed. Murdoch stroked her greying hair, keeping his eyes on Sorcha as she fought back tears herself. She could not bear to look at her mother, that much was clear. "A w-wedding and a child," Margaret continued, "wouldn't matter if the bairn was a b-boy or a girl. William was so good with children."

Something inside Lachlan twisted and coiled like a snake readying to strike. Whilst Murdoch was still a kelpie he could not father children with a mortal...but his final five years as a magical beast were up. Lachlan and Ailith had promised to change his very being permanently, and faeries always kept their promises.

There was just one thing Lachlan had to ask of Sorcha before he turned Murdoch human.

Tonight, Lachlan thought, as Sorcha's green-and-blue eyes caught his for just a moment before he turned for the forest with his companions. In them he saw all the anguish she was keeping at bay for the sake of her mother. She would cry later, he knew, perhaps when nobody was around. Lachlan loved her for it – the strength she held for other people in place of herself – though he also despaired because of it. It was the reason Sorcha was currently in such a dire situation, after all.

But Sorcha had long since made her decision to save the Seelie king and the kelpie of Loch Lomond at the price of half her life. There was nothing Lachlan could do about it now, except approach his mortal love with his most demanding request to date.

Tonight, he thought again as Ronan led him back into the cover of the forest. Once well hidden from the mortals at the funeral the faeries collectively let their nondescript human glamours drop, resulting in a whole host of strange and magical creatures left looking more bizarre than usual due to their uncomfortable, sombre mortal clothes.

Lachlan tossed one final glance over his shoulder in Sorcha's direction, though through the dense cover of winter pines he could no longer see her. *I will ask her tonight, whilst there is still time left to fulfil the request.*

He knew that Murdoch would not like what he was going to ask at all.

Ailith had remained at Court whilst Lachlan attended William Darrow's funeral, though the pale-skinned faerie was nowhere to be seen when he returned to the Seelie palace. *Her new lover is keeping her company, no doubt,* he thought, wasting no time in requesting a jug of blackberry wine from a passing servant on his way to the throne room. Lachlan was happy for Ailith – truly, he was – but seeing her with another was not exactly something he'd wished to witness over the past year.

And so it was that Lachlan was somewhere past tipsy when a silent-footed servant crept into the throne room to inform him that Sorcha and Murdoch had arrived. He was still in his mortal funeral clothes – largely all black, a colour Lachlan rarely wore – and his shoulder-length hair was in desperate need of a comb, but he did not care.

For what were appearances, in the face of the woman who could see right through them?

"Send them in," Lachlan said as he waved towards the servant, but in the time it took for him to speak the door was pushed wide open by Murdoch, closely followed by Sorcha. The kelpie was similarly still in the clothes he had worn to the funeral, though against his dark hair and coal-coloured eyes the ensemble did not look out of place in the slightest.

Sorcha, however, had changed into a familiar, forest-coloured dress with an intricately embroidered bodice that Lachlan adored. She had released her hair from its pins, too, and had clearly brushed through it until it shone going by the soft and lustrous way it tumbled down her back. She was a sight to behold, even with the slight tinge of red rimming her eyes suggesting she had indeed cried in the hours since Lachlan left her father's funeral.

Now I feel an idiot for not making an effort with my appearance for her sake, Lachlan thought glumly, rubbing a lock of bronze hair between his thumb and forefinger. *Though I suppose there is naught I can do about it now.*

Murdoch was the first to speak when he and Sorcha stopped in front of Lachlan on his gilded throne. He preferred the thrones that sat on the plinth outside in the revel clearing but given that it was January it was altogether much too cold to host such a meeting beneath the stars.

"What was so important that you had to call us here today, fox?" Murdoch demanded, though his voice was soft and gentle. For Sorcha's sake, Lachlan assumed, though given the kelpie's usage of his favourite insult *fox* he had to wonder what the point was of changing his tone. Either way, it didn't matter; Lachlan had to pose his request to Sorcha regardless of what Murdoch said or did over the next few, all-important minutes.

However, now that he was faced with what he had to ask Lachlan found that he could not look at Sorcha at all. He straightened on the throne, smoothing a hand over his hair and hooking a finger inside the uncomfortably restrictive collar of his human shirt as his brain fumbled for the right words.

"What I have to say – what I have to ask of you," he

began, very slowly, "is no easy request. I am well aware of that. Yet I have thought on the matter at length over the past five years and find myself in a position where it would be detrimental to delay voicing my request any longer."

Murdoch frowned, deeply suspicious, though Sorcha's previously sad expression changed in a moment to one of curiosity. She closed the gap between herself and the throne to rest a hand over Lachlan's. Her skin was icy cold, sending a shiver down his spine. But the way Sorcha looked at him was warm and familiar and tugged at Lachlan's heart, forcing his request out of his mouth before he could do anything to stop it.

"Have my child."

CHAPTER TWO

Murdoch

The kelpie of Loch Lomond had lived for five hundred and thirty-five years. Five of those years had been spent under the guise of Murdoch Buchanan. They were, without a shadow of a doubt, the best five years he had ever lived.

And now they were over, marked by the impossible request Lachlan had just placed at the feet of the woman Murdoch loved more than anything.

"Have my child, Clara," the faerie said again, falling back on the false name Sorcha had used when she first met him. "I beg of you. Please. I do not ask this lightly."

Sorcha said nothing. She stood inches from Lachlan, utterly immobile. Murdoch wished he could see her face – to know how the love of his life had reacted to the Seelie king's words.

She can't possibly accept, Murdoch thought, shifting his weight from foot to foot as he tried to decide if he should say something before Sorcha did. *What Lachlan is asking is madness.*

"Why are you asking this of her?" he blurted out, no longer able to remain silent. "Why now?"

Murdoch expected Lachlan to scowl or snarl or tell him it was none of his business. Instead, the faerie broke his attention from Sorcha to stare directly at him. "You should know that it is difficult for faeries to conceive a child," he said. "Our women give birth so infrequently, and it is a dangerous process. Having a babe with a human is the sensible option. And if I am to have a child with a mortal, then..." Lachlan returned his gaze to Sorcha, an enchanted smile on his face. "I would give up most anything for that mortal to be you, Sorcha Darrow."

"So you waited until my five years were *up* before posing this question to her?" Murdoch asked, beyond indignant. "Are you really so intent on getting between me and Sorcha that you—"

"It was precisely *because* I did not wish to interfere with your relationship that I had not yet asked," Lachlan cut in, a familiar lashing of venom colouring his voice. Murdoch scowled, intending to thoroughly disagree, but the faerie held up a hand to quell his tirade before it could begin. "I am being serious," he said. "With every year that passed with no interference from Eirian – and barely a word of gossip about the goings-on of the Unseelie Court – I realised all of us were only creeping closer to the moment when he might take her. No matter my opinion of you, horse, you clearly make Clara happy. Who was I to get in the middle your life together?"

Murdoch merely glared at him, for Lachlan *had*

gotten in the middle of his and Sorcha's relationship on several occasions. The two of them would by lying in bed together, content to do nothing but listen to the sound of wind and rain battering the walls of the Darrow house. Then, in the minute space between one moment and the next, Sorcha would be fast asleep.

It wasn't difficult to work out who was responsible for her sudden unconsciousness and inevitable, enchanted dreams.

Murdoch never asked Sorcha what she got up to in such dreams, nor had he ever confronted Lachlan about them. He knew it was not his place to pry; Sorcha and her fox had a complex relationship that Murdoch would never understand. But he *did* understand that Lachlan was important to her, and she to him.

He had taken to breaking his human form to go hunting in the loch whenever Lachlan invaded Sorcha's dreams, desperate to wipe the contented look on her sleeping face from his mind. Sometimes Murdoch would run into the Unseelie ghoul who had once granted him twelve hours as a human when his bridle had been stripped from him, thus saving his life as he knew it. They would hunt together, swimming close to the shore in order to lure unsuspecting humans out for evening strolls or midnight trysts to their waiting teeth and the mortals' inevitable doom. They would see who could do it the fastest, or the stealthiest, or with the most flair.

When Murdoch returned to the Darrow house after such hunts he always felt just as guilty as Sorcha looked upon waking up. They both knew they were indulging in dangerous impulses that they were not supposed to indulge. Yet despite those rare nights of madness the two of them had lived five unfathomably happy years, even taking into account William Darrow's increasingly ailing health.

And so it was that Murdoch could not help feeling glad that at least Lachlan's interferences had remained in the realm of Sorcha's dreams, and that their conscious interactions had been purely platonic. It was only listening to him now that Murdoch realised Lachlan could easily have taken things much further purely because he could. Alongside the fact that faeries could not outright lie, Murdoch had to conclude that the Seelie king was currently telling the truth about having not asked his ridiculous request of Sorcha at an earlier date.

"A child," Sorcha murmured, finally breaking her very long silence. She moved from Lachlan's throne to sweep around the room, eyes thoughtful and very faraway. Murdoch resisted the urge to rush to her side. She glanced at Lachlan, who stood as if on command. "You never mentioned wishing to have a child before. You are still very young by faerie standards, are you not?"

He nodded. "I never thought I'd want one at this age, admittedly. But you are twenty-seven, Clara, and in the blink of an eye you will be forty, then sixty, then gone. If I cannot have you happy to live forever then grant me the miracle of a child to remember you by. I would love them more than anything else in the world."

Again, Murdoch knew he had to be telling the truth, though it was plain as day from the look on Lachlan's face that he sincerely meant every word he said. A pang of sympathy ran through him, for of course Murdoch knew that the faerie loved Sorcha. Eirian might have stolen half of her life but at least Murdoch would get to live the other half of it with her, ageing alongside her –

dying alongside her.

Lachlan would never have that.

The Seelie king fidgeted uncomfortably when Sorcha continued her tour of the throne room in silence, tawny hair flashing copper down her back whenever the flickering light of a torch caught it. When the faerie threw a glance at Murdoch he promptly looked away, for he did not know what to say or do.

"You do not need to make a decision right here and now," Lachlan said, the words spilling out of him so quickly that Murdoch almost laughed at the faerie's uncharacteristic display of nervousness. "Take all the time you need. But please—"

"I'll do it."

"You'll – what?"

Both Lachlan and Murdoch stared at Sorcha as she finally came to a stop in the middle of the room, a determined glint in her eye that was completely at odds with the red-rimmed evidence of her grief over her father's death. "Of course I'll have your child, Lachlan," she said. "I would have done so even without your half-dozen reasons for why you believe I should."

Lachlan's face broke into a gleeful, sharp-toothed grin; he rushed forward and swept Sorcha off her feet, twirling her around and around until she was clinging onto him for dear life and the two of them were laughing. Murdoch took half a step towards the pair before thinking better of it. This was not something he should be part of.

Yet still Murdoch wished he was.

Eventually Lachlan placed a dizzy, stumbling Sorcha back on her feet and kissed the crown of her head. "Can you give me a few minutes with the horse, Clara?" he asked. Sorcha nodded and dutifully exited the throne room, though not before giving Murdoch the smallest of smiles that promised they would talk about everything later.

As soon as Sorcha was gone the atmosphere in the room grew tense and electric. "How bad is she getting?" Lachlan asked, eyes on the grand double doors as if Sorcha were still standing in front of them.

"She spends more and more time simply looking out of the window, but not at anything in particular," Murdoch replied, moving over to Lachlan's throne to lean against its side. All of his energy seemed to be leaking away at an alarming pace, as it always did with he and Lachlan discussed Sorcha's deal with the Unseelie king.

Lachlan finally tore his eyes away from the door and returned to his throne, slumping into it as if he felt exactly the same way as Murdoch, which he likely did. "Have you asked her what it is she's looking at...or looking *for*?"

"Every time. She says not to worry – that she is looking for nothing."

"You do not believe her?"

"Of course not."

A silence stretched between the two of them as they mulled over what this meant. Then, because he had heard no mention of it for a while, Murdoch asked, "Any news from your wizard friend? The one you hoped might be able to help us out of this?"

Lachlan shook his head. "Even knowing that Genevieve is a princess in France has not helped me in locating Julian. I fear we are running out of time."

Murdoch said nothing. To admit to the same fear aloud was to acknowledge that Eirian taking Sorcha away was real.

"If Sorcha does not get pregnant with the next two years then I will give up on having a child," Lachlan murmured, watching Murdoch out of the corner of a golden eye to see how he would react. "I do not wish to take more time away from the two of you than that. Ailith and I can still turn you mortal now, if that is what you wish, or—"

"I will wait," Murdoch said, certain. "If Sorcha is to carry a babe then I need to be able to protect her as best I can."

A flash of approval crossed Lachlan's face. "Good. I was hoping you would say that. Now go find Clara and help her grieve her father in a way that I cannot."

Murdoch did not need to be told to look after the woman he loved twice.

CHAPTER THREE

Sorcha

"You do not have to do this simply because you feel obligated, Sorcha."

Sorcha did not look away from the drawing room window, even when Murdoch perched himself on the arm of her chair and squeezed her shoulder. "I do not feel *obligated*," she said. "I want to do this."

A pause. And then: "I know. I just wanted to be sure."

The drizzle from earlier that day had turned into an all-out storm the moment the sun set. Sorcha peered through the darkness at the turbulent loch, listening to every crash and slap and groan the waves made as they slammed against the shore. She had encouraged her mother to drink several drams of whisky to help drown out the noise and ease her into sleep an hour earlier, and though Margaret Darrow had insisted she would find neither sleep nor solace in the bed she had shared for thirty years with her husband, but fifteen minutes later she had collapsed into an exhausted sleep.

Sorcha sincerely hoped the woman would be blessed with dreams of her husband in his heyday, when William was strong and young and illness did not plague him.

"The storms are not your doing, are they?" Sorcha asked Murdoch, though she knew he could no more control the weather than she could.

He chuckled softly. "It feels that way, sometimes. But I am not in so bad a mood tonight to cause a storm, my love."

"Even after Lachlan's request?"

When Murdoch slid down to sit beside Sorcha she made room for him, resting her head against his shoulder after a moment or two. He began to stroke her hair the way she liked, and she sighed contentedly.

"I cannot pretend that I am happy about what he asked of you," Murdoch said, "but I do at least understand. It is a kind and gracious thing for you to do, Sorcha, even if..."

"Even if you wish it was *our* child I was having," Sorcha finished. She looked up at him, craning her neck until she could graze her lips against Murdoch's jawline. It was dark with a shadow of stubble, but Sorcha enjoyed the sensation of it against her mouth. Murdoch's impossibly black eyes watched Sorcha's every move like a hawk.

She smiled. "We will have a family, I swear it. When I have borne Lachlan a child I will do the same for you – for us – and our little world will be happier for it. And just think!" Sorcha chuckled, more to herself than to Murdoch. "I will then have one mortal and one immortal child. Siblings. What are the odds they'll get on as well as you and Lachlan?"

Murdoch snorted at the notion. "I perish the thought of being more involved with the fox than I already have to."

"You would be brothers, almost."

"Now you are teasing me for the sake of it."

"It makes a difference from *you* doing all the teasing," Sorcha said, snaking a hand around the back of Murdoch's neck to bring his lips down to hers. He eagerly complied, wasting no time in deepening the kiss as he ran his fingers through Sorcha's hair.

A rumble of thunder broke the kiss a moment later; Sorcha immediately shifted her attention back to the window as if Murdoch was not sitting beside her at all. In truth she could see nothing through the pitch black of the stormy night, but it did not matter.

"When you and Lachlan have a child then neither of you will be alone, even when I am gone."

Sorcha was barely aware of what she was saying, nor of Murdoch's grip on her wrist as he tried to regain her attention. When he attempted to turn her back to face him she blankly resisted.

"Sorcha—"

"Carrying on their family lines is the only way mortals can truly live forever," she continued, voice eerie and disturbingly sing-song even to her own ears. "You and Lachlan will be fine. And I will be back before you know it."

"Sorcha, what is it that you aren't telling me?" Murdoch pressed, trying once more to turn her around to face him. He was successful this time, though the searching look he gave Sorcha turned to one of disappointment when it became clear she would not – or could not – answer him.

With a sigh he got to his feet. "Please speak to me," he said. "Or Lachlan. As much as I hate it, if it's him you have to talk to then talk to the Seelie king. Only do not keep what is happening to you inside your head. We want to help."

Murdoch paused then, waiting for Sorcha to reply. It took everything she had in her to say, "I think I would like to be alone, to grieve for my father," before returning to the dark expanse of night behind the windowpane.

She did not hear the kelpie leave the room, but part of her heart stung at his absence. It was her own fault, Sorcha knew. She was pushing both him and Lachlan away, bit by bit, and she could do nothing to stop it. There was an impulse – a voice in her head, almost – urging her attention to somewhere else.

Someone else.

That was when the raven appeared.

The bird appeared like clockwork, using the cloak of night to flit in and out of Sorcha's vision. It had become a regular fixture during the last five years of her life, appearing whenever Sorcha was feeling particularly sad or angry or confused. But it also appeared in moments when she was contented – when her life was easy and relaxed and she had could all but forget her deal with the King of the Unseelie Court.

All around her the shadows in the drawing room began to flicker and change.

Sing, girlie, they said. *Just one song. You are cruel to keep it from us for all these years.*

Sorcha did not reply, though a song was on the tip of her tongue dying to be released. She clutched her throat with desperate hands, begging the notes and words to stay firmly where they were.

"You are the cruel one," she whispered to the raven. Finally, the supernaturally large bird perched on the window ledge to tap on the glass right in front of Sorcha's face, watching her with eyes of unearthly silver instead of midnight black.

Sorcha touched the glass where the raven's beak had tapped it with the tip of her index finger. "Tell him that if he wishes to bother me here that it is time taken from the half of my life he holds claim to."

The bird cawed as if it was laughing. It sounded disturbingly familiar; nightmarish memories of dancing around and around on bloody, aching feet as mortal musicians played their fingers to the bone filled her head.

A song! the shadows called. *A song to dance to! A song to cry to! A song to die to!*

A single, delicate tear ran down Sorcha's face. "Leave me alone. Please leave me alone."

She knew deep down in her soul that they never would.

CHAPTER FOUR

Lachlan

Lachlan was nervous. More nervous than he'd been when he'd watched the kelpie behead his stepbrother and it did not break the fox curse the faerie had placed upon him. More nervous, even, than when an enchanted mortal woman had been sent to taunt Lachlan with riddles about Sorcha and the danger she was facing in London. Lachlan was, in fact, more nervous about tonight than he had been when he asked the question that directly led to what would transpire in the hours to come.

But the feeling was warranted; tonight was the first time Lachlan and Sorcha would actually go through the motions of trying to conceive a child.

Outside of her dreams Lachlan had not touched Sorcha the way he'd constantly longed to over the past five years. It had been difficult to resist whisking Sorcha away to the Seelie Court whenever he missed her most. But Lachlan was no fool, and he had grown up more in the past seven years than he had in the preceding ninety-seven.

She chose to live a mortal life with the kelpie, who was willing to give up all his power to be with her. That is not a relationship you interfere with.

And yet Lachlan *had* interfered despite this, on nights when the air was restless and everyone was dancing and laughing and losing themselves in each other at revels. He would sneak away from such events to his favourite room in the palace, deep underground and protected by a heavy iron door. There Lachlan would collapse into a pit of pillows and think of Sorcha, and within a matter of minutes he'd fall asleep and there she would be.

Lachlan knew Sorcha never told Murdoch about what the two of them got up to in her dreams, though often all they did was lie in each other's arms and talk for hours upon hours. Five years ago Sorcha's dreams had been full of splendid sunsets and golden lochs and jewel-coloured rain which never quite touched Lachlan's skin; since then, however, cold silvers and flickering shadows and blinding flashes of light had begun creeping in from every direction.

The last time he had been in Sorcha's dreams she'd been as distant as Murdoch had described her being whenever she sat by her drawing room window. It was this one, specific moment that had urged Lachlan to ask Sorcha to bear his child and heir, though he was worried he'd already left it much too late to broach the subject.

By the look in Murdoch's eyes as he watched Sorcha tell Lachlan that she *would* fulfil his request, he could only conclude that the kelpie very much believed there wasn't enough time left for her to have a faerie's child.

Lachlan shook his head; he couldn't afford such concerns to colour his mood right now. He had to ensure he looked perfect for Sorcha's arrival, and right now he could not decide what to wear.

"It will all come off soon enough," he mumbled at his reflection in the intricately carved, bronze-framed mirror that took up much of an entire wall of his chambers. Lachlan picked at the frilly collar of the white shirt he'd pulled on over his head, wondering if he should abandon it in favour of wearing his favourite green-and-gold robe over his bare chest, instead.

A flutter of nerves and excitement filled his stomach once more at the mere thought of being naked with Sorcha, limbs entwined and drenched in each other's sweat. The handful of times they had lain together in her dreams simply could not compare to the feeling of her skin beneath Lachlan's fingertips in real time. He imagined her cheeks flushing as he unlaced her dress, eyes never leaving his as he cast his gaze from her wild, unruly hair all the way down to her feet.

"Are you really faltering over what to wear, Lachlan?"

Lachlan jumped in fright at the interruption, grabbing his robe from his bed to hide the obvious physical proof of his impure thoughts. Ailith merely laughed her bell-like laugh as she glided into the room and easily folded herself into a chair by the fireplace. Her impossibly straight, pale blonde hair reflected the flames like a mirror, setting every strand alight.

He scowled. "Have you ever heard of knocking?"

"Have you ever heard of having ears with which to listen to your door opening?" Ailith countered. "Come sit with me for a minute."

Lachlan glanced at the door. "Clara will be here soon."

"And you do not wish her to see me in here with you?"

"Not directly before she spends the night, no," he replied, averting his eyes when Ailith snorted into her hand.

"Where did this sense of decency come from, Lachlan?" she asked. "You never cared about her knowing we were together before."

Lachlan leaned against one of his tall bedposts. He closed his eyes for a moment, pinching the bridge of his nose in the process. He was not sure he knew how to vocalise his current feelings. "This is...different," he ended up saying. "I feel uneasy. Nervous. I haven't – Clara and I haven't—"

"Ahh," Ailith cut in, understanding dawning on her fair face. She smiled sympathetically and rose to her feet, smoothing out non-existent creases in her long, silken skirt as she did so. "It was unfair of me to come here without taking your feelings into consideration. But you have kept a lot to yourself recently, Lachlan; it has not been easy to read you."

He shrugged. "You have been busy. I have not wished to burden you with my decidedly mortal woes."

"That is *exactly* what you should do, you fool," she said, closing the distance between them in an instant to gently kiss Lachlan's cheek. Ailith's next words were a whisper against his skin. "No matter how many lovers we take I am your queen, and you are my king. We have always been a good pair. And we will remain a good pair, until the end of time."

Lachlan bent his head, resting his brow against Ailith's as he sighed. "Do you think your consort is the faerie my mother prophesied?" he asked. "The one you were meant to be with in the end?"

"Lachlan—"

"I know, I know," Lachlan interrupted, quickly moving away from Ailith to browse sightlessly through his wardrobe. "It does not matter. But I hope he is, all things considered. For you to find him so soon, when you are both so young and with hundreds of years ahead of you...I am happy for you."

Ailith said nothing. She didn't have to; they both knew what was really on Lachlan's mind.

"Your Majesty. She is here."

Lachlan turned at the sound of the servant's voice, glancing at the door and then at Ailith as he fought against his now desperately beating heart. It was too late to fuss over clothes or Ailith's lover or any other matter that could possibly arise in the next thirty seconds.

"I shall go," Ailith said in hushed tones, reaching the door in three swift, easy strides. She gave Lachlan a radiant smile. "Good luck, my king. Try to remember to enjoy the evening."

As she left his room with the servant Lachlan almost laughed. Almost, but he couldn't force the sound out of his mouth. A vulpine bark was emitted instead, and Lachlan winced. *I shall never be allowed to forget my time as a fox, will I?* he thought, hurriedly running a gilded comb through his hair as the familiar sound of human-heavy footsteps reached his chambers.

"You are early," Lachlan said, taking a moment to collect himself before turning to face the woman who was currently closing the doors of his room behind her.

A pause. "Is being early a problem?"

When finally Lachlan *did* turn he forgot all about his nerves immediately. For there she was, the mortal he loved, dressed in a burgundy slip of a dress that must surely have been crafted by the silk weavers of his own Court. It hardly covered anything at all; Lachlan could see every curve and line of Sorcha's body beneath the fabric. Her hair was all loose tendrils around her face and shining waves down her back; a small smile curled the corners of her lips, which had been stained berry red.

"I thought it would be prudent to dress for the occasion," Sorcha said, not a hint of human modesty to be found in her voice. She took a step towards Lachlan. "But the faeries worked their magic faster than I thought they would, so—"

"Not a problem," he sputtered, too quickly, rushing to close the gap between them as quickly as he could. Lachlan slowly cast his gaze up and down her body just as he had imagined doing so five minutes earlier. "Being early, that is. That dress, however...now that *is* a problem."

Sorcha's mismatched eyes glittered in the low light of the room. When she brushed her lips against Lachlan's it was all he could do not to throw her to the floor in a flurry of mad, reckless lust. "Then how about we rectify said problem?" she asked, very quietly.

Lachlan's hand found hers, and he laced their fingers together. When he moved towards his bed Sorcha eagerly followed him. "That sounds good to me," he said, as he lay upon the bed and pulled Sorcha down on top of him. He kissed the skin below her ear, and along her jaw, until finally he found her mouth.

He bit Sorcha's lower lip. "That sounds very good to me indeed."

CHAPTER FIVE

Murdoch

Over the past five years Murdoch had tried his level best to live completely as a mortal. On nineteen occasions, however, he had succumbed to the primal desire to swim through the loch and search for lost souls to devour. Nineteen evenings of returning to his true skin; of feeling the rush of cold, dark water against every fibre of his being as he called out for prey.

Today marked the twentieth occasion.

"I wonder if the ghoul is about," Murdoch wondered aloud, rolling a crack out of his left shoulder as he prepared to dive into the loch. Three days had passed since Lachlan asked Sorcha to bear his child and Murdoch had later struggled to maintain Sorcha's attention for longer than five seconds as she sat by the window.

He had been concerned that night, as he lay in bed and waited hopelessly for her to join him, that this was the end for Sorcha. That Murdoch would awake the next morning and find her gone, spirited away to live half her life with the Unseelie king. But when the weak January sun rose and half-heartedly flooded Sorcha's bedroom with pale, wintry light Murdoch was relieved to find the woman in question curled up beside him, and when he roused her from her sleep Sorcha had been herself again.

She had not once sat by the window since then, though Murdoch caught her stealing glances at seemingly innocuous objects whenever she thought he wasn't watching. The objects were usually reflective, or cast long shadows, and every time Sorcha looked at them Murdoch's heart grew tight.

Eirian is watching her everywhere she goes. If Lachlan cannot find his wizard friend – or if the man can do nothing to help us – then Sorcha is doomed. I am doomed.

But, for now, the matter of the Unseelie king's claim on Sorcha was not the primary issue taking up all the space in Murdoch's head. For tonight Sorcha was going to stay in the faerie realm, and what she did with Lachlan in her dreams those past nineteen evenings would become very much a reality once more.

Do not be jealous. Do not be jealous. Do not be jealous.

There were faeries who granted wishes when they were recited three times, Murdoch knew; he wondered if any of them were listening to him right now. The relationship between himself, Sorcha and Lachlan could not be judged by mortal nor kelpie standards, for there was nothing simple and monogamous about it. But such a relationship was normal by *faerie* standards.

Though Lachlan loved Sorcha he continued to love

Ailith, too, despite Murdoch recently learning she also had a new paramour. And Sorcha had never had an issue with this – not even when Murdoch had been out of the picture, a prisoner in his own loch. Lachlan may have hated that Murdoch had since managed to win her heart, but the faerie had not once tried to stop Sorcha from being with him.

"Which means I am the only one who needs to get over my jealousy," he muttered. "I am the one who needs to change."

On this particular evening, however, Murdoch had no intention of getting over it. *No,* he thought, as he waded through the frigid loch and gladly leapt beneath the waves when it was deep enough to accommodate him, *tonight is for funnelling all my negative thoughts into a hunt.*

Murdoch swore it would be the final time he did so. But, unlike faeries, kelpies could lie.

*

"Something awful must be filling your head, to have drowned three people tonight so far."

Murdoch was quick to gather his dissipated form back together to face who had spoken: the Unseelie ghoul. The witch, for lack of another word.

He had learned over the past five years that the ghoul was female. She was a bizarre, ugly creature, with midnight-coloured, weed-like hair, disconcertingly large, metallic eyes and silver skin akin to fish scales. Her claws were honed to deadly points, as were her teeth. Even the ones that had broken were sharp enough to rend through flesh and bone.

She flashed those evil teeth at Murdoch. "Hello,

kelpie. Penny for your thoughts?"

"I think not."

"And here I thought we were friends!" she cried, twisting this way and that all around Murdoch with practised ease. He whipped out his tail and hit her in the face, though the Unseelie promptly avoided the attack in a flurry of bubbles.

"That you cannot lie makes that comment even worse," Murdoch bit out testily, annoyed that she had managed to evade him.

She pouted – or, at least, Murdoch thought that was what she was doing with her broken, twisted mouth – then turned herself upside down and swam in front of Murdoch's face. "I don't believe you do not think of me as a friend. I have helped you more than anyone, have I not? And I know you enjoy our hunts together."

"Friends have names, of which you seem disinclined to tell me yours. I thought it was humans who had to be wary of giving their names to faeries, not the other way around."

The Unseelie giggled. It was a disgusting sound. "That may be so, but I am also a witch. There are creatures darker than you or me that could do great and terrible things with my name...if there is any power left behind my name at all."

"Any power left?"

"Oh, kelpie, if only you had seen me in my heyday!" the creature exclaimed, dramatically falling deeper into the loch for several feet before returning to Murdoch's side in the blink of a gleaming, unnatural eye. "What a pair we would have been. I was quite beautiful, before."

"All your kind are beautiful, until they are not,"

Murdoch countered. "And you can glamour yourselves to look however you want, anyway. Superficial beauty matters naught to me."

"That is part of what makes you so formidable. You cannot be charmed or controlled by that which has vanquished generations of mortals and faeries alike."

Murdoch growled impatiently. "If you do not have a point—"

"I do, I do!" the faerie insisted. "I like you, kelpie. I like your home, and that you allow me to live here. It is the only kindness I have known for a long time. So I will grant you a kindness in return, if you only tell me what is on your mind."

Murdoch regarded her carefully. Faeries could not lie, but they could conceal their motives with well-spun words and flowery language. The Unseelie in front of him, however, could ultimately do nothing with the knowledge of what was bothering Murdoch. It was worth the risk of telling her what troubled him simply to see what sort of 'kindness' she would bestow upon him.

He let out a long spray of bubbles in lieu of a sigh. "Miss Darrow agreed to bear the Seelie king a child. She is with him now to...begin the process. I do not want to appear bothered by it for her sake, but it is vexing to say the least."

The silver creature grinned. "I already knew."

"Then why make me say it?" Murdoch demanded, snapping his teeth at her.

"Because we are friends! And now I know you are willing to talk to me. It means a lot, when part of your punishment is silence from your own kind."

Had this been any other day Murdoch would have

been genuinely curious about the faerie's past. Considering his current circumstances, he could not bring himself to care.

He huffed in her general direction. "What is this kindness that you promised me, then?"

"Oh, it is very kind and very good, I swear it," she said, bobbing up and down in the water as she spoke. "I saw something about you and your Miss Darrow."

If Murdoch had been in his human body he would have frowned. Instead he sharpened his form once more until he was large and solid and threatening against the comparatively tiny faerie. "What do you mean, you saw something? As in a prophecy? Or a vision? Or—"

"It is the kind of *saw* that is certain. Would you like to know of it?"

Murdoch could tell from the creature's deformed face that she was enjoying herself. All supernatural beings enjoyed teasing others, after all. It was simply that those 'others' were usually mortal.

He thought carefully about his answer before replying. The Unseelie swore what she had seen was good, and that it was certain, which meant that Murdoch knowing about it would not change fate. "Go ahead," he relented, after a minute of silence.

The faerie's bulbous, metallic eyes went glassy almost immediately. "Eighteen months and a day," she announced, in a voice that took Murdoch starkly aback by how beautiful and frightening it was. "Eighteen months and a day shall pass, and the kelpie will be granted a son from the woman he loves most dearly. Eighteen months and a day, not a second more nor less."

Murdoch struggled to process what he'd just heard. *A...son?* he thought. *A son! Sorcha and I are going to have a son. But eighteen months is not long at all. Will she – could Sorcha possibly bear Lachlan a child in that time frame, too? It does not seem likely.*

The faerie's prophecy changed everything. Knowing he and Sorcha would have a child together – a family together – so soon caused Murdoch to no longer care that she was currently with Lachlan. *Let them try their best for his sake. If Sorcha can deliver a child for him, too, then we will all be better for it.*

"A child for you both, so that you will never be alone," the Unseelie sang in her usual, garbled voice, interrupting Murdoch's train of thought. Her eyes were no longer glassy and faraway.

Murdoch stilled. "What did you say?"

"He has ears with which to hear," she said, propelling herself forward until Murdoch could no longer see her in the dark, murky water even with his exceptional vision. But her voice echoed all around, taunting him. "He can hear her, and then we all know. News like this never stays quiet long in the faerie realm – even for those of us no longer welcome there."

And then the Unseelie was gone, leaving Murdoch with a dozen new thoughts with which to wrestle. He twisted and turned on the spot for a moment, conflicted over what to do, before surging through the loch in the opposite direction to the faerie.

"Just one more soul and I am done hunting," Murdoch said, lying.

CHAPTER SIX

Sorcha

There was something dark and desperate about the way Lachlan touched every inch of Sorcha's body and held her close. She knew there had been more to his obvious nervousness when she'd first appeared in his chambers. A mania lurking beneath the surface, perhaps, or a madness.

Lachlan made no attempt at hiding such feelings now.

"I have missed you," he murmured, the words tickling Sorcha's ear when they brushed past her skin. Their clothes lay forgotten on the floor, their hair in equally wild disarray. When Sorcha rolled onto her back Lachlan rested his head against her chest with a contented sigh.

She stroked the length of his pointed, golden ear. "I have missed you, too."

"So why did you never approach me outside of your

dreams to—"

"Lachlan."

There was a warning in Sorcha's voice, but a sadness, too. It wasn't that she hadn't *wanted* to get lost in the arms of the Seelie king in her waking moments. Sorcha imagined she would never be able to stem such feelings. Yet she loved Murdoch dearly. She loved the kelpie with everything she could give him – everything but the love she held for Lachlan. Murdoch had told Sorcha, before, that kelpies loved but once and deeply.

They were completely different from faeries.

Murdoch tolerated Lachlan creeping into Sorcha's dreams, though she could see how much it cost him to do so. Each and every time Sorcha found herself knocked out by the faerie she awoke to discover Murdoch looking furtive and guilty; it did not take her long to work out what he'd been doing whilst she was unconscious.

Does he hate being a kelpie, or does he hate thinking that I might disapprove of what he is doing as a kelpie? Because I could never do that. Or...does he hate how much he relishes returning to his original form?

The last possibility hurt Sorcha the most, and made her feel ever more guilty. *She* was the reason Murdoch was giving up everything that he had been for five hundred years. His power. His proverbial freedom. His identity. And yet here she was, in the arms of the Seelie king.

A silence stretched between Sorcha and Lachlan, then, during which neither of them moved. But then the faerie started tracing circles across her chest, and her stomach, and her thighs, and he sighed.

"I understand," he said. "Of course I do. I only wish..."

"That Murdoch was a faerie?" Sorcha suggested, a frown creasing her brow. The pleasurable haze that had enveloped the two of them mere moments ago disappeared in an instant, leaving Sorcha feeling irritable and defensive. "That his approach to love and lust was the same as your own people? Or do you wish that he was not around at all, or that I did not love him? Or—"

"Sorcha, Sorcha," Lachlan cut in, the use of her true name causing her to stop mid-rant. He sat up, shaking his hair out of his face before looking down at Sorcha with desperately sad eyes. "You know that is not what I meant. If I had not accepted the horse by now I'd have tried to ruin your relationship long ago."

And then, as if it had never existed in the first place, Sorcha's anger blew away like a dying candle. She rolled onto her front, burying her face in a silken pillow before muttering, "I know. I'm sorry. I do not know what came over me. It was not my intention to ruin this evening for us."

It wasn't, of course. For with Murdoch's acceptance and understanding of the situation, and Lachlan's desperation to have a child, and her keen desire to give them both as much of her as she could *whilst* she still could, Sorcha had been looking forward to tonight.

But something was eating away at her brain.

Sorcha knew what it was even as she wished she didn't.

"He said you have been growing ever more distant," Lachlan said, stroking Sorcha's hair before trailing his fingers down her spine. She squirmed beneath his touch, and though it should have been pleasant the sensation was ruined by Sorcha imagining Lachlan's elegant fingertips belonged to someone else.

"The kelpie, I mean," Lachlan continued, when Sorcha made no attempt to reply. "I can see that what he speaks is true. Where are you right now, Clara? Where is your pretty head?"

"Away with the faeries," she replied, so wryly that both of them laughed despite themselves. She turned her head to peek a look at Lachlan out of the corner of her eye. "It is getting worse. I want to tell Murdoch but... I can't. Something is compelling me not to. It's funny... I've tried to tell you before - in my dreams - but I've never been able to. So why now?"

Lachlan considered this for a moment, scratching at the down-soft layer of stubble that covered his jaw. He chewed on his lower lip - a habit Sorcha was fairly certain the faerie had developed from her - then gasped when he came to a conclusion.

Sorcha pulled herself into a sitting position, deeply confused. "What is it, Lachlan?"

"When you are dreaming...I always thought, because it was an enchanted sleep, that if anything was creeping into them then it would do so here, but—"

"What on earth are you talking about?"

Lachlan grinned, a glint of hope in his molten eyes that Sorcha had not seen in months. "When you are dreaming you are still in your house," he explained. "A mortal house. Still susceptible to the magic and influence of Eirian. But in the Seelie Court - in the palace - my magic is strong enough to keep it out. I cannot believe I did not realise sooner!" He reached for

Sorcha, grabbing her shoulders and shaking them out of sheer excitement. "Tell your horse, Clara – the both of you are moving here for the time being!"

Sorcha could only gape at him. Lachlan's solution made sense, of course, especially if she was going to carry his child. But then she thought of the kelpie, and she grimaced.

"Murdoch is going to simply *love* this."

CHAPTER SEVEN

Murdoch

When Sorcha broke the news to Murdoch that they were moving to the faeric realm – the Seelie Court, no less – he had been furious. But after both she and Lachlan explained to him the reason behind the move Murdoch had no choice but to reluctantly accept.

Eight weeks later he could only conclude that the two of them should have moved there years ago, though Murdoch missed the Darrow house and it was very much clear that Sorcha did, too. But gone were her glassy eyes, vacant expressions and long stints looking out of the window with barely a word to say that made any sense.

Sorcha was more *herself* that she had been in at least two years, and for that Murdoch was eternally grateful. So what if he had to live surrounded by creatures he hated? He would gladly do it...for her.

In truth Murdoch did not hate *all* of the inhabitants of the Seelie Court. He had grown more than tolerant of Ailith over the years. Fond of her, even. The faerie was gentle and sensitive in a way far more befitting a human than a faerie, and she always spoke to Murdoch without disdain or fear or hatred despite the fact he had beheaded her once-future-husband. And he liked Ronan, Lachlan's ram-horned adviser to the throne, who was level-headed, liked to drink and held the Darrows in the highest regard.

Though he would never admit it, Murdoch found himself feeling safer within the Seelie Court than he had been outside of it. Seeing Sorcha finally relax and let her guard down only solidified his opinion that living with the faeries was the best thing for them.

At least for now.

"What are you thinking about, kelpie?"

Murdoch glanced up from his dinner – a feast of venison, blackberries and fat, buttered root vegetables that put most mortal meals to shame – to find Ronan collapsing down on the wooden bench beside him. The horned faerie looked exhausted, though his movements were just as agile as ever as he stole the largest chunk of venison from Murdoch's plate. The look Ronan gave him dared Murdoch to object, though he had no intention of doing so.

"I am merely thinking how Miss Darrow living here can only ever be a temporary measure," he said, granting the faerie the pure, unbridled truth. He speared a crisp-edged potato and chewed on it, only continuing to vocalise his thoughts once he had swallowed it in its entirety. "Tell it to me straight, Ronan: how long do you think we can hold off Eirian's attempts at reaching her?"

Ronan drank from a water skin attached to his belt, grimacing at the taste. He indicated towards Murdoch's goblet of dark, heady wine. "May I?" he asked, but before Murdoch had the opportunity to nod his assent Ronan had already begun drinking from it. When a servant passed by they dutifully handed Murdoch another goblet, though the faerie was quick to take that one, too.

"Bring us a jug," Ronan ordered, wiping his mouth before stretching his burly arms above his head. He let out an enormous yawn. "It has been long, exhausting work, ensuring the Court is protected to the standards set out by the king."

Murdoch did not take that as a good sign. "So you are saying we do not have long."

"On the contrary, we have needed to do this for many a year," Ronan said, surprising him. When the servant reappeared with a jug of wine the faerie eagerly took it and poured Murdoch a new measure of the stuff, thrusting it at his chest with brusque efficiency. "The Guard are exhausted, granted – I'm sure you have worked that out already – but we need to be pushed. To be trained. Queen Evanna ruled us for a long and fruitful time, and then she married the Unseelie king's half-brother. Clearly the idea was to unite the factions to maintain the peace she had worked for. However..."

"Eirian does not want that," Murdoch finished. "Do you think he can break through to the Seelie Court?"

Ronan's face was grave. "I will not lie to you, kelpie – even if I could, I would not. Your lady promised King Eirian half her life, so half her life he shall have. All you are doing is claiming your right to as much of the other half as you can whilst she is still young and beautiful."

Murdoch had not thought of it that way before; he had always, somewhat foolishly, believed that he and Lachlan could find a way to circumvent Eirian's claim and free Sorcha from her promise. Now it was looking as if that had never been an option, and never would be.

He stood up.

"Kelpie...?" Ronan wondered, eyeing him curiously.

"If I have but limited time with Miss Darrow then I should be spending it with her," he replied, inclining his head politely towards the faerie before rushing to the rooms he shared with Sorcha as fast as he could. The Unseelie witch in Loch Lomond was inside Murdoch's head again, taunting him with her intoxicating prophecy of a son.

Eighteen months and a day, she said. It has been almost two months since then; if this prophecy is as certain as she claims then I must become mortal and Sorcha pregnant – with my child, not Lachlan's – within the next seven months. What if a year and a half is all I get with her before – before –

Murdoch's manic train of thought was cut off as he became aware of the sound of retching. Anxious and hesitant, he paused outside the door to his and Sorcha's chambers to listen to what was going on, though ended up knocking upon the door before he could think better of it.

"Sorcha?" he wondered aloud. "Sorcha, are you—"

"C-come in," she sputtered, voice muffled by the thick wood of the door. "I am fine."

"You do not sound fine," Murdoch replied as he bowled into the room. By the fireplace sat Sorcha, shoulders hunched and arms curled around a wide metal bucket. A fine sheen of sweat covered her brow.

"I swear I—" she began, but then her eyes grew wide and she threw up into the bucket.

Murdoch rushed over, kneeling beside Sorcha to sweep her hair out of her face. "What have you eaten to cause such a sickness? You were fine earlier on."

When Sorcha finally stopped vomiting she let out three long, trembling breaths. She glanced at Murdoch for but a moment. "I have been like this for days now, though I have been lucky the nausea has hit me when you are in meetings with Lachlan."

"*Lucky?*" Murdoch bit out, incredulous. "Sorcha, what could possibly be lucky about—"

"I'm pregnant, Murdoch."

He froze.

Pregnant? If she is pregnant now, but has just seven months in which to carry the child before she becomes pregnant with mine, then...will she lose this baby? What was missing from the witch's prophecy?

But Murdoch could say none of this to Sorcha. Instead he forced a smile to his face, kissed her brow and said, "We must tell Lachlan. He will be thrilled."

He wished he had no reason to believe the Seelie king's happiness would be short-lived.

CHAPTER EIGHT

Lachlan

As Lachlan stared at Sorcha laughing and dancing away with Ailith he was struck by the realisation that he had never been as happy as he was in that precise moment. Everyone he cared about was close at hand, and safe, and *celebrating.*

I am going to be a father.

Lachlan would never have thought himself the type to possess a paternal instinct before. Even after he'd made the decision to ask Sorcha to bear him a child he hadn't been at all certain that he'd develop one. But now, with the knowledge that a baby was indeed on the way, all Lachlan could think about was being a father.

"My mother would not believe her eyes, to see me like this," he murmured, readjusting the delicately-woven golden circlet he was wearing to keep his hair securely away from his face. Lachlan stretched languorously, revelling in the comfort of the pit of pillows he was currently using as a throne, having ordered the iron-doored, underground room typically used by him in the late, late hours following a revel to be turned into a paradise befitting Sorcha for the evening.

All around soft, glowing lights floated from place to place, lazy and slow as if they were heavy with sleep. The air smelled of lilacs, bluebells and pine, for garlands of flowers and sweet-smelling berries were strung from every nook and crevice in the stone walls, and shelves of rock had been covered in fine cloths and a plethora of food and drink.

Lachlan had worked his own magic upon the bubbling, merry burn that snaked across the room, lending it an internal glow to match that of the phosphorescent mushrooms that grew in clusters alongside spears of gemstones in a multitude of colours.

A small fiddle band played in the centre of the room, having removed the cushions and blankets from the largest pit to turn it into a recessed stage. Around them all manner of Seelie danced and sang; Lachlan felt his entire being relax simply by watching them.

He was content. He was happy. He didn't want the night to end.

When Sorcha caught his eye she beamed, her face luminous in the green-and-blue light currently enveloping her frame. She did not wait for Lachlan to wave her over to break from her dance with Ailith to collapse beside him in the pit. Sorcha made to kiss Lachlan's cheek, though he turned his head just enough that her lips landed upon his own, instead.

"Fox!" came Murdoch's warning cry immediately, as if he had been standing behind Lachlan the entire time waiting for him to do something offensive; Lachlan would not have been surprised if that had indeed been the case.

The kelpie was quick to sit down by the edge of the pit, cross-legged and cross-armed and looking particularly unamused. But there was a flush to his cheeks that suggested Murdoch was tipsy, and his shirt had been undone to his navel.

"You look as if you've been more salacious than I have, horse," Lachlan said, wrapping an arm around Sorcha to pull her in closer. But she merely giggled, sliding out of Lachlan's grasp to sit precisely in the middle between him and Murdoch before grabbing both of their hands.

"The two of you must learn to get on," Sorcha insisted. She glanced at Murdoch. "You have enjoyed living in the Seelie Court, though you would never admit to it aloud. And Lachlan – you feel safer knowing you have a kelpie on your side, and you know it. Murdoch has proven again and again that he is trustworthy. So can't the two of you just be...friends?"

"Absolutely not!" they both bit out, which only made Sorcha laugh harder.

"You cannot say I have not tried, at least. Murdoch, why are you so dishevelled, anyway? Did that water nymph try and seduce you again?"

Lachlan barked at the notion. "Someone other than Clara found your dark and moody countenance attractive enough to proposition you *more* than once? I do not believe it."

"Murdoch Buchanan is a ladies' man," Sorcha said, grinning at Murdoch's murderous expression. "A real Lothario. Clearly even as a dead one he is irresistible to all manner of women."

"I think she hoped I might grant her part of the loch," Murdoch admitted, running a hand through his curly hair as he did so. Lachlan noted it was growing well past his ears again and wondered, not for the first time, if the kelpie himself decided whether his hair and stubble grew or whether it happened naturally.

I truly know nothing of the creature, Lachlan thought. *Perhaps it would not be a terrible idea to at least learn more about Murdoch in the years to come.*

"I thought you had already granted a faerie part of the loch," Sorcha said, starkly removing Lachlan from his own head.

He frowned at Murdoch. "You have? A *faerie?*"

"An Unseelie ghoul hardly counts as a faerie," the kelpie replied, flashing a look at Sorcha that screamed *Why did you tell Lachlan about that?*

Lachlan forced back a shiver at the notion of an Unseelie ghoul. They were foul creatures, and if this one lived in Loch Lomond instead of the faerie realm, then...

"Did they tell you why they were in your abode?"

Murdoch grimaced. "No, but from the little I have learned I do not imagine I want to. She was a witch, though, and a powerful one, so I imagine she performed some kind of unforgivable magic."

"And how have you come to—"

"If the two of you are going to discuss this until it becomes an inevitable argument then I shall continue dancing with Ailith," Sorcha cut in, turning first to Lachlan to kiss his cheek and then to Murdoch, who kissed her brow instead, before leaping out of the pit with a spryness Lachlan would not have expected from a pregnant woman.

Though she is not that far gone yet, he reasoned. *Now that the sickness has passed she will have a few weeks of respite before her belly truly begins to show.*

"Everyone believes it is Ailith who is pregnant, yes?" Murdoch asked the moment Sorcha disappeared, sliding down from his perch to sit as close to Lachlan as he could clearly bear.

Lachlan forced himself into a sitting position, sighing heavily. "Must we ruin this one evening of happiness with talk of the danger all of us are in?"

The kelpie did not answer; his dark eyes said everything Lachlan needed to know, though they were bleary from alcohol and faerie fruit.

He scratched his ear where his mother's bell-like, silver earring used to be. "Only my inner circle knows. Most everyone in this room believes Ailith to be the one carrying my child, yes. Which was difficult to pass off, given that we cannot straight-out lie."

"And you have quelled the rumours for why Sorcha and I are staying here?"

"The entire realm knows about her deal with Eirian, horse," Lachlan said, rolling his eyes. "They believe you are both here to try and stay away from him, which is the truth. What more could you want?"

Murdoch crashed onto his back, falling heavily through a flurry of pillows. When he resurfaced he looked throughly resigned. "For there to be a permanent solution to our problems," he said, so quietly Lachlan almost missed it. "I would live within the Seelie Court forever if it meant Sorcha never had to go to him."

It was Lachlan who did not have to reply with words this time. To have Sorcha live within his home for the rest of her life was all Lachlan had ever wanted. Even if that life was a mortal one. Even if it included a kelpie who had once tried to steal his throne – and his face.

With a long, slow stretch Lachlan got to his feet, then held his hand out to help Murdoch up. "Come," he said. "I fear Ronan will drink all the wine if we do not take some for ourselves."

The kelpie looked at him suspiciously. "We are not seriously becoming friends, are we? I cannot stomach such a thought."

Lachlan grinned a grin full of sharp teeth and devilish intent. "No, but we are comrades whether we like it or not, and as such I intend to show you how easily I can out-drink you."

"That sounds like something I can perhaps agree to," Murdoch said, pushing aside Lachlan's hand in order to stumble to his feet on his own, "though I most assuredly will be the one to out-drink *you*. I am a giant, monstrous horse, after all." He glanced down at his mostly-undone shirt as if considering buttoning it back up again, then shrugged and left it the way it was.

Comrades, Lachlan mused. They passed Sorcha and Ailith, who delighted in the sight of the Seelie king and the kelpie of Loch Lomond in each other's company without a fight breaking loose. *I can cope with comrades. It would make Sorcha happy, too.*

After all, that was all Lachlan wanted, and that was what she currently, undoubtedly was.

He did not want the night to ever end.

CHAPTER NINE

Sorcha

Within the underground revel time stood still, but deep inside Sorcha's bones she knew it was very, very late indeed.

Or early, as the case may be, she thought. *This is the faerie realm, after all.*

The celebrations were beginning to die down, faeries dropping where they stood to collapse across blankets and cushions and each other. Some of them were doing far more than simply sleeping, their soft laughter and sighs of pleasure from the shadows the only hint Sorcha needed to politely look away from their salacious activities.

In one corner lay a drunk and unconscious Murdoch, half-hidden in a mound of cushions with an exhausted but contented smile upon his face. Sorcha bit back a laugh at his dishevelled hair, wine-stained lips and unbuttoned shirt. He had lost his shoes at some point in the evening, and the ends of his trouser legs were wet, suggesting that he'd waded into the ethereal burn winding across the floor like a luminous serpent.

Sorcha had not seen the kelpie so relaxed in months – years, even. It hurt her heart to think of what her promise to the Unseelie king had done to him. But Sorcha could not regret saving Murdoch's life at the expense of half her own. Could *never* regret it.

She loved him more with every passing day. That he was alive because of her was perhaps Sorcha's greatest personal achievement.

"Would you like some sugared plums, Miss Sorcha? Miss Sorcha?"

Sorcha blinked in Ailith's general direction. It took her a while to spot the faerie, for she was nestled in the crook of her consort's arm. He was taller and broader than Lachlan – similar to Murdoch in stature – with soft brown hair and eyes to match. Sorcha vaguely recalled talking to him earlier in the evening and liking him well enough, though she found she could no longer remember their conversation.

She could not even remember his name.

I feel hazy, Sorcha thought. *I must be tired.* But the haziness felt different to exhaustion. Familiar, in a way Sorcha did not wish to acknowledge.

"No thank you, Ailith," she said, remembering to answer the faerie's question a moment too late. But if Ailith noticed Sorcha's obvious distraction she did not comment on it, choosing instead to beam at her before feeding her lover a sugared plum from the woven basket sitting on her lap.

A few minutes later both Ailith and her brown-haired companion fell into an easy sleep, so Sorcha drifted across the room following the path of the burn. It was then that she noticed Lachlan, snuggling a small mountain of cushions as if they were leaves and he was still a fox. His cheeks were rosy, his smile soft and innocent.

He looks so young, Sorcha thought. *Too young to be a father.*

But Lachlan had one-hundred-and-four years of life experience, whilst Sorcha had a meagre twenty-seven. Even taking into account that Lachlan was still a relative youth in faerie terms, she had no doubt that he would make a good parent. In the seven years that Sorcha had known him he'd demonstrated a willingness to learn, grow and compromise that was unrivalled by any human she had ever met – including her own father.

She placed a gentle hand across her belly, thinking of the child growing inside her.

"*O can ye sew cushions,*" Sorcha murmured. A lone fiddler sent her a hopeful glance, lifting up his bow as if to join her song, but Sorcha merely shook her head and he lowered it, disappointed. *I will sing the full song to the babe when I feel their first kick,* she decided.

Sorcha had never imagined herself the maternal type; until perhaps a year ago she hadn't once considered the possibility of having children. But the thought of raising a family with a human Murdoch – to pass on the Darrow name to a new generation – had been too beautiful a dream to pass up. That Sorcha was now in a position to do the same for Lachlan brought her a happiness she could not put into words.

She gazed down at her stomach. Soon she would begin to show, and then the pregnancy would have to be kept hidden from the rest of the Seelie Court. Sorcha was no fool; she knew how important it was to stay safe and protected within the bounds of Lachlan's magic until the babe was born. To be taken by Eirian before then would be immeasurably dangerous.

"If you are a boy I will name you..." Sorcha began, but then she froze. She felt as if something was choking her, forcing her to keep her babe's name secret. Sorcha swung around wildly, wondering what was wrong. Behind her the lone fiddler began to play a heart-wrenchingly sorrowful melody.

That was when the shadows began to flicker.

Nobody else still awake seemed to notice them or, if they did, passed off the strangeness as a side-effect of faerie wine and revel madness. But Sorcha could see them. Could *hear* them.

No, she thought, stricken. She turned this way and that, intending to rouse Lachlan or Murdoch or Ronan and his guards, who should never have fallen asleep but were dozing together against a wall regardless, heads drooped low over their chests.

Leave them, a silky voice ordered, *and follow me.*

It was a voice Sorcha had not heard in five years. A voice she wished somehow to never hear again, despite her promise to the creature to whom it belonged. Though the voice had not spoken aloud, it felt very much as if it had come from behind the heavy iron door that prevented all but the most powerful faeries from entering and exiting the room.

But Sorcha Darrow was not a faerie.

Holding her hands over her ears, Sorcha tried desperately to retreat further into the underground room and away from the door, all the while flashing pleading glances at a group of nymphs who were somehow still awake. But they ignored Sorcha, choosing instead to continue dancing to the fiddler playing his ballad. With every note he coaxed from his strings Sorcha's feet insisted that she should follow the terrifying, seductive voice that had spoken to her.

She stumbled across the burn, feet away from Murdoch. *Just scream,* Sorcha thought. *Scream or kick his shoulder and he will –*

Follow me, the voice commanded once more, and Sorcha dropped her hands. She took a step forward. Another. Two more. Five. Before she knew it Sorcha was unlocking the door, fingers shaking as she fumbled with the lock and slid out of the room without so much as a glance back at Murdoch and Lachlan.

Sorcha tried to yell out but she couldn't make a sound. She tried to drag herself to a halt, or claw her nails across her skin to force a cry from her lips, but she had lost all control of her body. She walked up the heavy, carved stairs that led to the ground floor of the palace and glided down the corridors as if pulled by an invisible piece of string.

Very pale morning light filtered through unshuttered windows, causing Sorcha's eyes to water. She blinked tears away until she grew accustomed to the light, just in time to reach the grand front doors of the palace.

I cannot open them, she realised, a surge of relief washing over her. *They are too heavy. Just so long as—*

The doors swung open.

When Sorcha peeked outside she saw that one of the guards had opened them for her; before her very eyes he grew sleepy, then passed out on the gem-encrusted pathway.

How has he broken through Lachlan's magic? Sorcha wondered, horrified, as her feet resolutely marched her off the path and into the forest. The air beneath the trees was dark, wintry cold and entirely untouched by the morning sun. The grass and moss all around her was covered in frost, and it occurred to Sorcha as the ice stung her skin that she was barefoot.

Closer, the voice said, much louder this time. *Just a little closer.*

Sorcha had no choice but to grit her teeth against the cold biting at her hands and feet and face, the skirts of her gossamer and silk faerie-spun dress trailing behind her like fog rolling off the loch. Along with her wild hair, wide eyes and pale cheeks Sorcha half-imagined herself a ghost as she continued through the silent forest.

If you are a ghost then disappear, she thought, wishing she could close her eyes. *Disappear, and everything will be fine. If he cannot see you then he cannot find you.*

But such thoughts were in vain, and as Sorcha came across a clearing lit by a singular, slanting ray of light her heart grew heavy. For standing there in front of her was her doom, and she was walking right towards him.

He was dressed in regal, smoke-coloured armour shot through with starlight, and sat upon a dappled grey mare with soft eyes, a wavy mane and a calm, pretty face. With his winged, silver helm, braided hair and flowing white cape the King of the Unseelie Court looked every inch a knight in shining armour, the kind of which featured prominently in the stories Sorcha used to delight in reading with her father.

Except the faerie was no knight, and he was not here to save her.

A resplendent villain, Sorcha thought, taking a step towards the faerie despite herself, *but a villain nonetheless.*

"Come," King Eirian said, whisper-quiet. His mercurial eyes never left Sorcha's as he held out a hand to help her onto the back of his horse.

Sorcha had no choice but to obey his command.

The last thing she was aware of thinking before the Unseelie king urged his horse to hurtle through the forest, Sorcha clinging to him for dear, terrible life, was that she had not had the sense to tell both Murdoch and Lachlan that she loved them at the revel.

As a single raven feather fell from the heavens above, something deep inside Sorcha became certain she would never get to say such a thing to them again.

CHAPTER TEN

Murdoch

When Murdoch awoke his body was sore and his head was groggy. All around him the revel had died, with most of the attendants passed out in pits of cushions and silken sheets. He rubbed at his temple, the promise of a headache beginning to creep up on him, but Murdoch pushed it to the side for now.

How long was I out? he wondered, dragging errant curls of hair away from his face as he tried to work out how late it was. The soft, glowing lights that floated through the air before Murdoch passed out had whittled away to next to nothing, and the burn was no longer lit from within, but Murdoch's keen eyes were used to such darkness. The dull light from the phosphorescent mushrooms reflecting off quartz and topaz and tourmaline was more than enough for him to make sense of his surroundings.

Two pits of cushions to Murdoch's right lay a soundly sleeping Lachlan, on his back with limbs sprawled lazily around him. His bare feet were twitching as if he were chasing something through a dream.

Once a fox, always a fox, Murdoch thought, rolling his eyes before sweeping his gaze across the room. He spied Ailith in a corner, curled against the side of a tall, broad-shouldered faerie whom Murdoch now knew was her consort. Two members of Lachlan's guard were leaning against either side of a snoring Ronan, whose horns were stained with blackberry wine and decorated with twisting wreaths of ivy.

All of the musicians in the centre of the room were asleep, bar one, who was playing the softest melody upon his fiddle that Murdoch had ever heard. It was lulling the last of the revel-goers into unconsciousness, though a group of four or five nymphs insisted on dancing to the music even as they yawned and closed their eyes.

Everything was calm. Everything was quiet.

Everything was wrong.

There was no physical evidence to point to such a wrongness but the kelpie did not need any. Murdoch could feel it in his bones. In his stomach. In his heart.

He staggered to his feet, bile rising in his throat that had nothing to do with the excesses of the revel.

"Where is Sorcha?"

Murdoch's question had been quiet, yet there was a thunder in his voice that carried across the entire room, silencing the lone fiddler and halting the nymph dancers in one fell swoop.

A solitary golden eye became visible in the corner of Murdoch's vision; he turned to face Lachlan just as the faerie rolled over and leapt to his feet. The delicate circlet upon his head was at such a haphazard angle that the moment Lachlan took a step towards Murdoch it fell to the floor with a clamour. The sound echoed all around them, reverberating off the stone walls and returning to Murdoch's ears as a distorted, unsettling mockery of the original jingle of metal on stone.

Lachlan sniffed the air, ears pricked up to attention. He narrowed his eyes at Murdoch. "When did you see her last?"

"I do not know," he admitted, waving a hand uselessly around him. "You were still awake when I fell asleep. How long have you been unconscious?"

The Seelie king considered this for a moment, waving over Ronan and the two members of his guard who had been snoring softly but a moment ago. "What time is it?" he asked.

"Close to eight in the morning, going by the sound of the birds above us," one of the guards replied. The creature had huge, owl-like ears; clearly being underground was no barrier to them being able to hear the goings-on of the forest. They inclined their head politely at Lachlan. "You have not been asleep long, Your Majesty. But an hour or so. Queen Ailith was still awake with Miss Darrow at the time."

"And then what?" Murdoch demanded, stealing the words before Lachlan himself could ask the same question. "Where did she go? Why were you asleep when she was still awake?"

"I—" the owl-eared faerie glanced at their partner, then at Ronan, who grumbled as he tore away ivy from his horns.

"We do not know why we fell asleep," Ronan said,

answering for all three of them before either Lachlan or Murdoch had an opportunity to lose their temper. His eyes were bleary in a way that had nothing to do with alcohol.

Lachlan glanced at Murdoch. "He was here. He was *here*. In the Court."

"He might still be," Murdoch said, wasting no time in heaving open the iron door that nobody but Lachlan and Ailith could open.

Lachlan roused his queen with a gentle touch of her cheek; Ailith's eyes opened immediately. "Sorcha is missing," he said. Murdoch hated that he could hear a waver in the faerie's voice. "Search the east side of the palace with Ronan. The kelpie and I will take the west."

Lachlan did not give Ailith a chance to reply before he rushed out of the door with Murdoch in tow. The palace was deathly quiet; all Murdoch could hear was his and Lachlan's heavy, foreboding footsteps as they rushed down corridor after corridor. Early spring light filtered through the windows, painting the golden walls with heartbreakingly beautiful sunshine.

Too beautiful for this particular morning, Murdoch thought. *There should be rain. There should be a storm. There should be darkness.*

When Lachlan made an about-turn and veered towards the entrance to the palace Murdoch stumbled over his feet in shock. "You sense something?" he asked, watching the Seelie king as the faerie darted his eyes in most every direction.

His nose twitched. "I can smell her. She went outside."

"Being a fox is good for something, at least,"

Murdoch said, the rising panic in his throat turning him towards useless conversation in order to keep his wits about him.

Lachlan threw a raised eyebrow his way before struggling to push open one of the enormous front doors. Murdoch moved forward to lend his weight to the endeavour, and when the door slammed open the sound of it hitting the palace walls awoke a guard, who was strewn across the gemstone-encrusted pathway as if he'd had too much to drink.

Murdoch helped the faerie to his feet. "How long have you been asleep?" he asked.

The guard furrowed his brows against the morning light. "I was asleep? I don't remember...Your Majesty!" he cried the moment he spied Lachlan. He hurried into a bow. "King Lachlan, I do not know why—"

"How long were you asleep?" Lachlan asked, repeating Murdoch's question in decidedly clipped tones.

"L-less than an hour, going by the sun," the guard stammered.

"Did you see Miss Darrow?"

"Miss Darrow? I – yes," he said, very slowly. Horror paled his face as he realised what he had just said. "Something compelled me to open the door for her, and—"

"Damn it!" Lachlan cursed, sweeping past the guard to venture into the forest, Murdoch close behind.

For twenty minutes neither of them spoke a word. Lachlan followed his nose, and Murdoch dipped his fingers into every burn and pond they passed. But the water-dwelling creatures he spoke to seemed to have no memory of the last hour; they had nothing of use to tell Murdoch.

Close to an hour later the kelpie had to admit that their search was fruitless. He had known, from the moment he awoke, that something was awry. Murdoch did not need a fox's nose or an owl's ears or a falcon's eyes to know what it was he knew.

He could not feel Sorcha anywhere.

When Murdoch came to a stop it took Lachlan a moment or two to realise he was not following him. The faerie paused, turning his head to look at Murdoch with an expression that screamed *do not say it.*

Murdoch said it anyway.

"She is gone, Lachlan. Sorcha is gone."

CHAPTER ELEVEN

Sorcha

The first thing Sorcha noticed about the Unseelie Court was that it was cold. The solstice revel she had attended five years prior had been attended by so many creatures that the bitter, winter air of the ancient ballroom had been kept at bay by a thousand bodies. Now she was surrounded by emptiness, and though it was near the end of March and spring had been upon the air back home Sorcha couldn't stop shivering.

All around her was eerie, suffocating silence as King Eirian slowed his grey mare to a halt in a cobblestone courtyard. Fog rolled across the stones, obscuring much of Sorcha's surroundings, but here and there she could see hints of a gargantuan, intimidating castle rising up to dwarf her very existence.

The horse let out several puffs of air, her muscles shuddering as the Unseelie king gracefully dismounted and held out a hand to help Sorcha off, too.

She did not take it.

"You cannot sit upon my horse all evening," Eirian said, chuckling softly as he removed his winged helm and shook his hair out of his face. "I have no doubt that you are tired, Miss Darrow, so come down and let me show you to your chambers."

For a long moment all she did was stare at him. King Eirian looked even paler and unnatural in the fog than he had done at the winter solstice revel, though Sorcha knew that it was her – not him – who was out of place. A faint sheen of sweat crossed the Unseelie king's brow; it brought out the blue undertones of his silvered skin, reminding Sorcha of fish scales beneath midnight waves.

Eirian frowned. "What are you thinking about, my mortal paramour? You have the most unusual expression on your face."

"I am – I am *not* your paramour," Sorcha bit out, indignant, finally breaking her silence. The words felt odd in her mouth; she had not spoken for hours and hours, though she had been screaming inside her head ever since Eirian stole her away from the Seelie Court.

A small smile flitted across his face. "Perhaps not. Perhaps I am getting ahead of myself. Either way, you must be freezing. Allow me to bring you inside."

Sorcha forced herself not to comment on the Unseelie king's presumption. With a flick of her wrist she swatted away his outstretched hand, gritting her teeth against her frozen muscles in order to slide down from the mare on her own.

The moment she dismounted a ghost of a faerie emerged from the fog to take the horse's reins, gently pulling the creature away until, in the space of a blink, she could no longer see the mare's soft grey hair nor hear her hooves clatter against the cobblestones.

When Eirian shirked off his thick, white cloak to drape it across Sorcha's shoulders she shrugged it off. "I do not need your false kindness," she said, marching forwards in what she hoped was the right direction. "You and I both know I promised half my life to you under duress. You are no gentleman, so do not act like one."

"You are bold, to speak to the King of the Unseelie Court in such a way," Eirian replied, tone entirely pleasant as he wrapped his hand around Sorcha's left arm to lead her towards the entrance to the castle. His talon-sharp nails dug through the sleeve of her dress to bite at her skin, though Sorcha resisted displaying her discomfort of the sensation on her face.

She did not look at Eirian as she said, "I see no reason why I should not say what I think to you. You cannot kill me, for doing so breaks our deal and frees Lachlan and Murdoch to destroy you. I do not imagine they would respond kindly to you torturing me, either."

Eirian's resultant laughter was so loud and gleeful that Sorcha flinched. It echoed all around the courtyard, even through the fog, and when the sound returned to Sorcha's ears it was warped and sinister.

The Unseelie king stopped in his tracks and turned to face Sorcha. His silver eyes flashed like knives, cruel and razor-sharp. "You have no idea what I can do to you, Miss Darrow," he said, tone as silky and dangerous as it had been at the solstice revel. "You are lucky I would very much prefer things remained civil between us. So civil, in fact, that you grow sick of it, and fall willingly into the Unseelie way."

"That will never happen," Sorcha replied, fighting to sound steady and unfaltering when in truth she was terrified. She had seen but a glimpse of the savagery of the 'Unseelie way' at the revel, and it was not something she ever wished to witness again.

Sorcha knew she would have no choice but to experience it again over the course of the next thirty years that Eirian owned.

The Unseelie king's mouth pulled into a smirk. "I am inclined to believe you," he said. "That is, in fact, what makes this entire deal so amusing. Now follow me, and let us get out of this cold."

So Sorcha followed him, for there was little else she could do. Momentarily she entertained the idea of fleeing simply to see what would happen, but ultimately Sorcha dismissed the idiotic notion. For she could finally think – and converse – properly; Sorcha could not remember a single prior encounter with the Unseelie king in which she had been in full control of her senses. She did not want to give him a reason to weave whatever magic was responsible for clouding her mind whenever he was around, or watching her through a raven, once more.

If she was going to spend half her life in the Unseelie Court, Sorcha Darrow would much rather be lucid and fully in control of herself. To lose her senses would spell doom, and it was not only her life that would suffer for it.

The baby, she thought, gulping back a sharp intake of breath as she finally *remembered* that she was pregnant. Eirian glanced over his shoulder at her as they ascended a helical staircase, but did not utter a word.

I have to be careful, she thought, a hundred times more anxious than she had been mere seconds ago. *He cannot find out. But how can I hide a pregnancy? I will begin to show soon. And then – and then –*

Sorcha could only pin her hopes on Lachlan, Murdoch and the members of the Seelie Court working out a solution to her impossible problem. Eirian had no claim to the baby, but he could just as easily kill the child the moment they were born. *But that will incite war. That will* –

"We are here."

When Eirian unlocked a large door made of ash and embellished with silver Sorcha hesitantly peered inside. The room was high-ceilinged and circular, with tall windows punctuating the stone facade facing east and west. Large swathes of the stonework were covered in tapestries; the floor was likewise adorned with all manner of furred and woven rugs.

A four poster bed larger than Lachlan's fit against the curve of the furthest part of the wall from the door. There was an obsidian fireplace built into a recess a few feet away from it; the flames within burned white-hot, chasing the chill from the air. Above the fireplace was a vast, frameless mirror, its edges clouded with age.

The smallest of touches on Sorcha's shoulder was enough to make her stumble into the centre of her new chambers.

Her prison.

"There is a washroom through there," Eirian said, waving almost lazily at a heavy maroon curtain that mostly obscured another ash door, "though the hot springs down below make for a far more pleasurable bathing experience."

Sorcha said nothing. She wondered if Eirian would simply leave her be if she remained silent, though when he turned her around to stare at her it became apparent that he would not.

"I suppose this is acceptable for thirty years or so," Sorcha commented, trying her best to remain unphased by the entire situation.

Eirian cocked his head to one side, silver-white hair flashing in the firelight as if it were made of stars. When he grinned Sorcha caught sight of his wicked canines, which were longer and sharper than Lachlan's. Everything about the Unseelie king was harder than his golden kin. Crueler. Sadistic.

It should have therefore come as no surprise to Sorcha when King Eirian raised an index finger to her forehead – the same one that had marked her with his blood five years ago, thus sealing her fate – and laughed very softly.

"Tell me: do you know what half of forever is?"

Sorcha's insides froze. When she tried to back away Eirian slid a hand behind her back, forcing her to stay put. "What are you talking about?" she asked, though Sorcha was not stupid. She knew exactly what Eirian was insinuating; it was simply that she could not fathom it.

It was the Unseelie king's turn to say nothing. A frown of concentration darkened his eyes, and all the laughter was lost from his lips. But a moment later his expression returned to one of amusement, and he lowered his finger from Sorcha's brow.

"It's said that when a human is turned immortal they steal their new lifetime from a faerie who was doing nothing with their own," he said, retreating towards the door as his eyes scanned Sorcha from her head to her toes. "So I wonder, Miss Darrow, that if there were some truth to the saying, who then might be the unfortunate creature from whom I stole their life to give to you?"

Something warm and faintly ticklish began to creep down Sorcha's inner thigh, followed by a spasm in her womb that she fought to keep to herself. Her heart was beating far too quickly, chest heaving in fear and horror.

No.

Oh, please, no.

Eirian smiled grimly, clearly enjoying the look of blank shock upon Sorcha's face, but he could not see the singular drop of blood that was beginning to run down the inside of her thigh that indicated she had lost something far more precious than her mortality.

"Enjoy forever, Miss Darrow," he cackled, closing the heavy ash door with a resounding slam as he left her new prison.

Blindly Sorcha rushed to the closest window ledge, though she could see nothing but fog through the glass. When another cramp hit her she collapsed, crumpling to the floor as she clutched her stomach and tried her hardest not to cry out. With every passing second more blood escaped her body, crawling and seeping down Sorcha's legs. She could do nothing to stop it; nothing to turn back time.

Sorcha Darrow's unwanted immortality had come at the cost of her baby.

CHAPTER TWELVE

Lachlan

Murdoch had barely made it into the throne room, dripping wet from his head to his toes, when Lachlan asked, "Anything, kelpie? Anything at all?"

The dark-haired man nodded his head, morose and exhausted. He had been jumping from loch to river to sea for thirty-six hours straight, looking for answers concerning Sorcha's disappearance. "A pair of selkies by Liverpool swore they saw Eirian upon the back of a grey horse, a woman in tow," he said. "An Unseelie near London said the same, though they did not wish to." A vicious, humourless grin spread across the kelpie's face, leaving Lachlan in no doubt about how the creature coerced the Unseelie to speak.

He tossed Murdoch a loaf of bread, which he enthusiastically tore into. Lachlan was just as tired and hungry as the kelpie was; he had spent much of the past day and a half scouring the forest and the outskirts of the Seelie Court for any witnesses to Sorcha's disappearance.

Unsurprisingly there were none, though a faun claimed to have spied a raven flying overhead for hours and hours before it vanished from sight whilst the revel celebrating Sorcha's pregnancy was going on.

Most likely Eirian himself, looking for a weakness in our defences. My *defences.*

Lachlan leaned against a nearby column of stone, sliding down to the floor as he let out a long, low whistle of air. "So Eirian broached through our defences on a horse. He sent everyone still conscious to sleep and lured Sorcha out to meet him without having to enter the palace or alerting me to his presence. Damn the forest!" he cursed. "I thought we might actually be strong enough. I thought we could keep him at bay until - until –"

"Until your mortal wizard appeared and told us he couldn't help us?" Murdoch cut in bitterly, following suit and collapsing to the floor beside Lachlan. He stole the wineskin from the faerie's belt, gulping down half the contents before unceremoniously flinging it back at Lachlan.

He caught it without looking at it. "He might have had a solution," Lachlan insisted, though his voice was weak and lacked conviction.

"Yet he could not help you with your fox curse," Murdoch pointed out. "I thought you said the wizard admitted to not being well-versed with curses?"

"This is not a curse, though; it's a promise made under duress. There's a marked difference between the two."

The kelpie clucked his tongue. "What could a human do to wheedle out of a faerie promise? Wizard or not, mortals lack the years of experience needed to deal with your kind."

"Oh, but he was very well versed with *my kind,*" Lachlan countered, bringing the wineskin to his lips and finishing what Murdoch had left for him. Though he knew the wine was deep and sweet and heady, Lachlan thought it rather tasted of ash and winter in his mouth.

"He had a way with words, my wizard," he added on quietly, thinking of Julian and his companion, Evie, with her hair spun from gold. "He knew what to say and what not to say to me. Do you know I owe him a favour for saving my life? If he can help us now I'll owe him a hundred of them, and gladly."

Murdoch thought about this for a long time. Eventually he said, "What if we can do nothing, Lachlan? What if Eirian's hold on half of Sorcha's life cannot be broken and—"

"She is carrying my *child,* Murdoch," Lachlan snapped, surprising even himself with his use of the kelpie's self-appointed name. "You think I would be able to rest, knowing that silver-skinned monster has - has—"

Lachlan couldn't finish the thought. He was ashamed to feel tears beginning to prick his eyes, so he turned his face away from Murdoch. *How could I have had a mere handful of joyous days before everything was torn from me? Sorcha, our child, our future...*

A silence stretched between the pair, during which time Murdoch wrung out his sodden sleevesr. For a few moments Lachlan listened to the water drip down to the floor. Then, because he realised his previous statement implied he only cared so much because of the babe in her womb, said, "I wouldn't give up on saving her even if Sorcha wasn't pregnant."

"I know."

Lachlan stilled. "You do?"

"Of course I do," Murdoch said, sighing heavily. Lachlan glanced at him; there were dark, purple-tinged shadows beneath the kelpie's eyes, making him look closer to death than to life. He looked haunted and hollow. Hopeless.

He looked exactly how Lachlan felt.

"I would be a fool to deny how much you love Sorcha," Murdoch continued, staring up at the ceiling with irises so black they seemed to absorb all the light from around them. "Just as you would be foolish to pretend my love for her does not run deeper than my love for the water – for my very being. And yet our feelings were not enough to keep her safe. If anything they were her downfall."

Lachlan considered this. *It is true Sorcha would never have become embroiled in all this had I never met her. But I cannot imagine my life without her in it. The kelpie must surely feel the same way.*

"Would you have revealed to her who you truly were, had I not shown up and interfered with your plan to act as Murdoch Buchanan?" he asked, genuinely curious.

The kelpie seemed surprised by the question. He ran a hand along his jaw, which was rough with stubble. "If I am honest I had not thought things through, at the time," he admitted. "I saw the man standing by the shore and acted on impulse. I'd only meant to consume him, not become him."

"But then you did."

He smiled. "I did, because of her. I wanted to meet her. I'd always wanted to meet her."

"So why *hadn't* you? You could have taken on the guise of most anybody to meet Sorcha."

"Like I said, I did not plan it," Murdoch replied. "I thought I was content merely watching Sorcha from afar. But once I *had* met her...well, I lost all such notions of leaving her side."

Lachlan barked out a laugh. "So we are in agreement, then?"

"In agreement?" Murdoch frowned, confused. "Agreement of what?"

"That there is no situation in which either of us could not have her in our lives. Which means there is little point in mulling over whether things might have been different, once upon a time."

And though Lachlan felt like he might drown in his feelings of loss and helplessness and fear, he knew he was right. Drinking wine and ruing their life choices would not save Sorcha.

He stood up, sending a wave of drying magic Murdoch's way. The kelpie winced as he always did when faerie magic touched him. "Come," Lachlan said, indicating towards the door with a nod of his head. "The envoy I sent down to the Unseelie Court might have returned by now, and Ronan has been hard at work figuring how we might find a way to *fight* Eirian, should we fail to save Sorcha through other means. I imagine such a plan is of interest to you."

When Murdoch flashed the same murderous, blood-drunk grin Lachlan had seen upon his face the night they stormed through the Unseelie solstice revel he knew the kelpie was more than on board with such a plan.

"I am glad I did not turn you mortal back when you first asked, all things considered," Lachlan said as the two of them wound their way through the palace.

Murdoch cracked his knuckles, chuckling softly.

"I am inclined to agree with you, fox."

CHAPTER THIRTEEN

Eirian

Forty-eight hours had passed since Eirian stole away that which Sorcha Darrow treasured most: her mortality. He had been waiting five years to take it from her, and now those five years were finally, deliciously over.

And forever was only just beginning.

The Unseelie king's haunting of her over the past half a decade had successfully isolated Sorcha from most everyone she loved, until she could hardly focus on anything but the foreboding presence of a silver-eyed raven.

When Lachlan had decided to move Sorcha to his Court Eirian had admittedly been irked. The young king's power grew with every year he sat upon his throne, and it had been no easy task for his silver counterpart to infiltrate the Seelie side of the faerie realm. But Eirian had managed it, and now he had the mortal who so foolishly promised half her life away in order to save the Seelie king and the dark, dangerous kelpie of Loch Lomond.

Now that Sorcha had lost her mortality, the unfortunate girl was a hostage Eirian could use until the end of time; a threat to keep both Lachlan and the water horse firmly in their place.

Beneath my feet.

"You have not moved an inch in two days, little bird," Eirian murmured, swirling a fingertip across the surface of the tall, mottled mirror through which he was observing Sorcha in her room. He could only see her back, for the mirror in her chambers was behind her, and though her stillness piqued Eirian's curiosity he had resisted visiting Sorcha during the past forty-eight hours. He had sent no servants to her with food or water or warm clothes, either, in the hopes of forcing the woman to leave the confines of her room of her own volition.

But Sorcha had not moved.

Behind him the crack of a whip and a wretched, high-pitched scream filled the air, curling Eirian's mouth into a cruel smile. He rose from the mirror, smoothing down the front of his shirt before sweeping across the torture chamber to face the source of the anguish.

A torn, bloodied slip of a faerie limply hung from her shackles. Beside her stood a pointed-nosed Unseelie, who sneered at her before snapping his long, leather whip across her chest once more. She was cut to ribbons; Eirian knew the unfortunate creature would be left with no skin at all once her torture was over.

The faerie was an envoy, sent by Lachlan to ensure Sorcha was untouched and in good health. The Unseelie king had no qualms, of course, about leaving him entirely in the dark on the matter of the safety of his human consort.

And flaying the yellow-gold faerie who had been sent to shed light on the matter.

"He should have sent nobody at all, until he had a promise from me that no messengers would be harmed," Eirian said, mostly to himself. It seemed like folly on Lachlan's part, though he reasoned the fox might simply be acting rashly over his fear for Sorcha's wellbeing.

She would be faring much better if she submitted to her fate and dared to leave her room, Eirian thought, leaving the torture chamber to head for the woman's room in question. In truth he expected nothing less from Sorcha than to be hard-headed and wilful; her choosing not to move even for food and drink and rest was not so impossible a decision. But it still felt odd. Wrong. Out-of-sorts.

Something was going on with Sorcha Darrow, and Eirian had grown impatient to discover just what exactly that was.

When he reached the door to her chambers Eirian paused, hand on the carved silver handle as he considered what he might do if the woman inside refused to speak to him. *I could cloud her mind as I have done before,* he reasoned, *though that takes a fair amount of concentration on my part...as well as diminishing how fun it is to tease and torment her.*

But when Eirian finally opened the door and took in the sight of Sorcha by the window all such thoughts vanished. For the pale, weightless material of her dress was bloodied around her thighs, and her expression was so hollow that for a moment the Unseelie king genuinely believed that Sorcha Darrow had killed herself. Then she blinked, and he breathed a small sigh of relief.

"What have you done, foolish lass?" Eirian asked, closing the distance between them to loom over Sorcha. The skin beneath her eyes had purpled like bruises; when she looked lifelessly up at him she looked more a ghost than a human.

"It is none of your concern," she croaked through lips that were as cracked and dry as her throat. Her bottom lip had split open, revealing a flash of scarlet blood.

When Eirian bent down to investigate what she'd done to herself Sorcha flinched away so quickly that he was taken entirely by surprise. He frowned. "I will not harm you," he said. "I merely—"

"Stay away from me!" Sorcha cut in, baring her teeth as if she were a trapped animal. Eirian supposed she likely felt like one, but he had no patience to deal with such behaviour. He grabbed at the skirt of Sorcha's dress, ripping most of it away even as she continued to scrabble away.

Eirian scowled. "All I want to do is heal whatever mess you've made of – oh."

Oh.

He had expected to see welts or cuts across Sorcha's thighs – evidence that she had deliberately hurt herself in retaliation for him spiriting her away and turning her immortal. There had been too much blood soaked into her dress for it to be explained away as the natural bleeding a woman experienced with every turn of the moon, after all.

But there were no cuts. No bruises. The blood had come from within her, spilling down her thighs until it dripped down onto the stone floor. For a moment Eirian did not know what to say, for he was not sure what was going on.

Kelpies cannot father children, he thought, staring hard at Sorcha even as she looked away, eyes too bright with the promise of furious tears. *And it was only just announced that Ailith was pregnant with the heir to the—*

"You were the one carrying Lachlan's child," Eirian murmured, voice soft and very gentle as he let go of the torn, bloodied material of Sorcha's dress to kneel by her side. Inside he was roaring with delight; he could not have asked for a better turn of events. There was no torture Eirian could imagine that would destroy his rival more than the loss of his own child.

But, for now, Eirian kept such gleeful thoughts to himself. Sorcha was one bad day away from madness, and he rather did not want her to stoop to such levels so soon. With a sigh he scooped the woman into his arms and got to his feet, tightening his hold on her when Sorcha struggled and pushed against his chest.

"Do not fight me," he warned. "All I am doing is taking you down to the hot springs to clean you up. You cannot languish like this for any longer."

"I can *languish* however I want," Sorcha choked, throat full of tears but otherwise dry as bone.

Eirian cast a glance at her, though Sorcha's green-and-blue eyes did their absolute best to avoid his gaze. She looked small and insubstantial in his arms, her bloodied, white dress making her look altogether like a sacrifice to the Christian devil, saved from the alter with but seconds to spare.

His mouth was a hard line as he said, "I will not allow you to sit there and wait to die. Either you clean yourself, feed yourself and get some sleep, or I will do all three for you."

Sorcha did not reply; it was clear from the look on her face that she did not like either option. When finally they reached the hot springs, however, a glint of interest lit up her face, and she pushed herself once more out of the Unseelie king's arms.

Eirian smiled as he let her go. "I had a feeling you would like it down here. Now, would you—"

"Leave me alone," Sorcha said, not looking at him. Her eyes were fixed on the scene in front of her: a dark forest, nestled in the very centre of the castle with the midnight sky high above it. Steam filled the air, snaking across the floor and around the trees, obscuring the actual hot springs from sight.

Eirian's temple twitched at Sorcha's insolent tone, though he merely gave her a mocking bow and retreated. "As you wish, Miss Darrow. I shall send someone down with more appropriate clothing for you."

Once more Sorcha did not reply, for she had already disappeared into the steam as if she'd never existed at all.

"A strange one indeed," the Unseelie king muttered as he turned and left the forest. "A strange one, and a difficult one, but I shall break her."

After all, Eirian loved nothing more than a challenge.

CHAPTER FOURTEEN

Lachlan

Lachlan did not notice Ailith, even when she bent low to plant a kiss on his cheek. It was only when she spoke hushed, soothing words into his ear that he realised he was not alone.

"I may have a way you can see Miss Sorcha."

He stared at her without seeing her; Lachlan had spent many a sleepless night trying to reach Sorcha in her dreams over the past three weeks to no avail. Not a single envoy he had sent to the Unseelie Court had returned, either, meaning Lachlan had no idea how Sorcha was or she was being treated. He knew that if he went down to speak to King Eirian the Unseelie king would almost definitely refuse to grant him an audience with Sorcha, and would instead likely use the opportunity to torment him.

Lachlan therefore could not fathom how Ailith had possibly worked out a way he could see the mortal woman he loved.

His assurances to Murdoch that they would work out how to save Sorcha and fight Eirian had fast become empty words; with no information coming through on the state of the Unseelie Court Lachlan, the kelpie and Ronan could not construct a sound plan of attack against the silver king. And there was still no word from Julian despite Lachlan's messengers finally locating the wizard's abode, for the man had not been home in some time. Every new blow resulted in a hopelessness seeping into Lachlan's soul which he could do little to quell.

I am running out of what few options I thought I had.

"Lachlan? Lachlan, are you listening to me?" Ailith asked, no hint of scorn or impatience in her voice. Her eyes were soft and gentle as they watched Lachlan's every move, though a frown darkened the lovely blue of her irises.

"I am, as always, open to any and all ideas," he finally sighed, collapsing into the embrace of a velvet-lined armchair that perfectly imitated the ones in the Darrow drawing room. He had grown fond of the chairs over the years; now that Sorcha was gone Lachlan found himself spending more and more time sitting upon his replica instead of his throne.

Ailith chuckled as she perched upon the armrest. "It is gratifying to see how much confidence you have in my idea," she said, "though given the current state of events I am inclined to forgive you."

Lachlan's only response was a pointed look.

Ailith swept his hair out of his face with careful, unwavering fingers. "How would you feel about being a fox for a few hours?"

"I – excuse me? A *fox?*"

"You heard me," Ailith said, a slow smile spreading across her face. "I have been thinking on it for a while – how you might creep into the Unseelie Court unnoticed. King Eirian only seemed able to broach *our* defences in the form of a raven, if the faun in the forest is to be believed."

"But we do not know for sure that the raven was—"

"Ah, but we have another piece of evidence that suggests it was," she cut in.

Lachlan furrowed his brows. "And what, exactly, is this evidence you speak of?"

"You."

His frown deepened. "I must admit that you have lost me, Ailith. What do you mean that *I* am the evidence?"

Ailith shifted from the armchair to stand in front of Lachlan. She placed her hands over his own, squeezing them in barely-contained excitement. "Seven years ago you stalked back into the Seelie Court in the form of a fox, and both Innis and Fergus did not notice."

"But that was because the kelpie was wearing my skin," Lachlan countered. "He—"

"Was still not *you*. That you were able to re-enter the Court without alerting anyone to the presence of a powerful faerie tells us that it is indeed possible to do so. It lends credence to the idea that Eirian was that raven. He only reverted to his true form once everyone powerful enough to stop him had been lulled to sleep. And if he can do that..."

"Then I can," Lachlan finished, no longer frowning. Ailith's idea was outlandish and dangerous, but it was also the best idea Lachlan had heard in weeks. He bit his lower lip as he thought things through. "I would have to remain a fox whilst inside the Unseelie Court," he murmured. "I do not have the talents someone as old as Eirian has in putting a hoard of faeries to sleep. He will notice my presence if I turn back into a faerie."

"Then it is a good thing Miss Sorcha is very familiar with your fox form," Ailith said. With a tug on Lachlan's hands she pulled him to his feet. "Come, there is no time to waste. Once you are transformed I can transport you to the outskirts of the Unseelie Court. The faster you leave the faster you can reach Miss Sorcha and check on her health...and the babe's."

Lachlan winced. He had tried his level best not to think about his unborn child, though he had not slept for longer than two successive hours because of the difficult subject. He trusted Sorcha to keep her pregnancy hidden as best she could. *But soon...*

Soon she will no longer be able to.

"The hor–Murdoch is still in the loch," Lachlan said, forcing himself to think of more than his own worries and desires for a moment. "Perhaps I should wait for his return in case he has any messages he wishes to pass on."

But Ailith shook her head. "He has been gone almost two days, Lachlan, and he did not say when he would return. I believe he would understand the urgency with which you need to reach Miss Sorcha."

Lachlan did not need to be told twice. "All right," he said, inspecting his gaunt reflection in a mirror before remembering that Sorcha – if he managed to reach her at all – would see him as naught but a fox. "All right. Let's do this. Turn me into a fox, Ailith."

*

Lachlan hardly had time to process Ailith's magic

before he found himself unceremoniously dumped on the shadowy outskirts of a thorny, wicked-looking briar of dead brambles. He rolled to his feet – disconcerted to discover how easy it was for him to ease back into having four of them instead of two – and snapped his teeth.

"Twelve hours and counting," Lachlan muttered, the words coming out as half a bark. That was how long Ailith could give him, though he doubted he'd need longer than that to find Sorcha. She would be in Eirian's castle, no doubt, and though Lachlan was not all that familiar with the place he *was* familiar with Sorcha's scent. With the nose of a fox it would be easy to track her.

He simply needed to stay hidden whilst he did so.

I should be glad for this fog, Lachlan thought, taking a few careful steps beneath the dark, twisted trees that surrounded the castle. *It will keep me concealed. But I mislike it nonetheless.* The fog was freezing, even through his fox fur, and when Lachlan tried to shake off the cold he became aware that he was growing damp.

"Wonderful," he growled, before deciding to remain silent for the rest of his search. A wily faerie would be able to sense that another faerie was nearby, after all, though they would have no idea how strong or important said faerie was.

Lachlan thought back to the cursed fox he had met seven years ago; he had been able to intermittently smell a faerie upon the air, because the poor creature was close to losing himself entirely. But Lachlan had only been able to track him because he knew he was searching for a fox that was not a fox; if an Unseelie sensed him now they would have no idea that the faerie they were aware of was hidden in the guise of an animal.

Which I must use to my advantage at every turn.

Over the course of two hours Lachlan traversed the thorny forest until he came upon the castle itself, sniffing at the cold, dead stones until he found several of them that were warm and teeming with life. Steam curled from the cracks between them, intermingling with fog and soaking Lachlan in condensed rainwater. He shook himself as dry as he was able to, nose to the ground as he searched for a weakness in the earth to grant him passage to the castle.

And then he heard it – the sound of running water, almost swallowed in its entirety by the fog. Lachlan skittered towards it, stopping when he reached a narrow burn crawling *out* of the castle through a small grille in the wall. Plumes of steam wafted off the water's surface, and when Lachlan placed a curious paw within it he found that the water was warm.

I can make it through there, he thought, cocking his head to regard the grille before burrowing between two of the bars. It was a struggle, though, and for one horrible, drawn-out moment Lachlan was sure he was stuck. But the sound of two perimeter guards approaching was the panicked impetus he needed to push through, and with a rushed exhalation he squeezed between the metal bars.

Lachlan held in a splutter of relief as he crept along the bed of the burn, keen eyes adjusting to the glum air with every step he took. Black pines and wispy willow trees surrounded him, turned ghostly with ever more steam. When the burn began to deepen Lachlan nimbly jumped out of it and followed its path, veering to the left when it began to widen into a pool. He could hear what sounded, bizarrely, like a waterfall in reverse, and Lachlan realised a moment before he saw it what was responsible for the noise.

A hot spring.

He had never been in this part of Eirian's castle before, though it did not surprise him that the king possessed such a lovely secret within his walls. Even in the height of summer the Unseelie Court was generally cold and foreboding; it made sense that there was at least one warm place in the castle at all times of the year.

Then Lachlan heard a splash, and he retreated into the cover of the trees. But he could not smell a faerie, though all the water around him made it difficult for Lachlan to smell anything at all. Curious despite himself, he edged back towards the water, sniffing this way and that until—

Sorcha. I can smell Sorcha.

Lachlan wasted no time in running around the water, following her scent as it got stronger and stronger until, finally, he caught sight of her. Sorcha was sitting below a willow tree, legs dangling in the steaming pool in front of her with her dress hitched around her waist. Her eyes were closed; her breathing slow. Lachlan wondered for a moment if she was asleep, but then Sorcha sighed and slumped her shoulders.

His heart ached to watch her. Her cheeks were gaunt and pale, and her collarbone protruded outwards more than it had done when Sorcha had been stolen away. Lachlan grew furious thinking about Eirian starving her, then pushed all notions of the Unseelie king away. He was here to talk to Sorcha about herself and their baby, not the villain who had taken her.

Lachlan wondered how to announce his presence to the mortal woman. His bushy tail twitched, and as he shifted his weight from his left paws to his right it occurred to him that he was nervous. *This is not the time for immature, human emotions,* he chastised, taking another step towards Sorcha. He shook out his fur again, causing it to stand on end before the steam curling all around him began to flatten it once more.

But Sorcha did not hear his silent approach, and with her eyes closed she could not see him. So Lachlan swallowed, pushed his nervousness to the side, and did the only thing he could think of doing.

He sang.

"But to see her was to love her;

Love but her, and love forever," Lachlan began, keeping his voice as soft as a whisper in a dream. Sorcha's eyes flew open, looking around wildly until she spied the orange fur and pointed nose of the fox mere feet away from her. She stared at Lachlan in disbelief.

"Had we never lov'd sae kindly," Sorcha replied, singing the next line of the song with a voice full of tears.

"Had we never lov'd sae blindly," Lachlan echoed back.

"Never met – or never parted –

We had ne'er been broken-hearted."

An insurmountable pause. And then –

"Lachlan!" Sorcha cried, crushing him against her chest when Lachlan leapt into her arms. She buried her face in his ruff, sobbing without restraint. "I couldn't – how did you—"

"I am a fox," Lachlan replied with a confidence entirely put on for Sorcha. "Of course I was going to find a way to reach you. But I fear we do not have long; I cannot risk being spotted. So tell me, Clara, how are you?" When Sorcha lifted her head she looked thoroughly miserable. Lachlan nipped at the end of her nose. "He is not starving you, is he? You look about ready to faint!"

"No, I – I have been given plenty to eat," Sorcha said, wiping away her tears with the back of a hand, "but I haven't had much of an appetite. I—"

"You have to keep your strength up, Clara!" Lachlan insisted. "Eirian wins if you are kept meek and submissive. And the baby—"

"I lost the baby."

"...needs all the – what?" Lachlan stared at Sorcha, not quite believing the last words to have been emitted from her mouth.

He was numb.

He was empty.

He didn't know what to do.

"What did you...the baby?" he said, though the words felt flat and useless. "You lost the baby?"

"I do not think – it was not my f-fault," she wailed, which crushed Lachlan's heart to hear. He could mourn later, on his own. For now he had to support Sorcha through her loss.

"Of course it isn't your fault, Clara!" he said, gently licking her tear-stained cheek and tasting salt. "There are always risks with pregnancy, and for faerie children even more—"

But Sorcha violently shook her head, cutting Lachlan off. "I do not mean it like that. I – Lachlan – *he* took our baby! He stole the child's life to make me immortal.

He...he means to keep me here forever."

Lachlan went limp in Sorcha's arms. For most of the past seven years he had longed for his mortal companion to willingly live forever with him – for her to *choose* to strip away that most fundamental part of her humanity so that he could love her until the end of time. But in the beginning he had not intended for Sorcha to be able to choose; he had wanted to use her full name to enchant her to his side.

Now that Eirian had taken Sorcha's mortality from her, Lachlan realised just how villainous his original intentions had been towards her.

"We will work this out," he said, though the words were empty. "There is a solution. We can—"

"But I cannot be turned mortal again, can I?" Sorcha countered. There was a darkness clouding her eyes that Lachlan hated to see. "The process is irreversible one way or the other. That was what you told Murdoch, was it not? When he wanted to be turned human."

Lachlan said nothing. It was true, and they both knew it. But he didn't want this to be how things ended – Eirian winning against him in the most wicked, underhanded way possible at the expense of Sorcha losing most out of everyone.

He rubbed his muzzle against Sorcha's face. "Do not lose hope yet," he whispered. "You saved me from my curse when the situation seemed impossible. Allow me to do the same for you, Clara. Please—"

Lachlan flinched; he could smell a faerie upon the air. Going by the way Sorcha stilled she had sensed the new presence, too.

"Go," she mouthed, kissing the top of his head for

but a moment before Lachlan slid out of her grasp and darted through the trees towards the grille in the wall. To his relief the faerie presence did not follow him, and when he escaped the warmth of the hot springs for the bitter chill of the fog outside he could no longer smell the creature at all.

Lachlan ran from the castle. He ran through the forest, and when he reached the bramble briars he ran some more. He did not stop running until his fox form finally dissipated and, even then, he continued on two feet back to the Seelie Court.

Every step away from Sorcha was worst than the last, and the further Lachlan got from her the more her confession weighed upon him.

Our baby is lost.

CHAPTER FIFTEEN

Murdoch

So much for living as a mortal, Murdoch thought as he ploughed through the loch. *I have spent more time in my true form than my human one ever since Sorcha was taken away.*

Murdoch had just returned from a five-day-long trip around the waters of Great Britain, scouring for gossip and scraps of overheard conversation that would give him a clue about how Sorcha was faring and what King Eirian was currently plotting. That none of Lachlan's envoys had returned from the Unseelie Court unnerved Murdoch to no end, and he could not bear to rest on his laurels and wait for news that may never come.

But the kelpie was exhausted from his journey – and starving. It was poor etiquette to hunt in another kelpie's territory, so Murdoch had not eaten for days. Now that he was on his home turf he was determined to fit in a hunt before returning to Lachlan and his Court, where he would doubtless be disappointed by the lack of news concerning Sorcha.

It is hardly as if I found out anything, either, Murdoch thought as he slowed his pace through the loch, drifting upon the lazy springtime currents to listen out for any humans taking advantage of the warm afternoon sunshine close to the shore. The water was still freezing, of course, for the snow sitting atop the mountains had finally melted into the loch, but Murdoch had found that the bite of the water did little to deter those most determined to swim.

A kick somewhere above his head and a squeal of delight alerted Murdoch to the fact that a child had jumped into the loch, closely followed be their complaining elder sibling. They were easy prey; for a starving kelpie there could be no better meal.

But they were children, and Murdoch had gradually lost his stomach for eating them ever since he began living with Sorcha Darrow. Now that Sorcha was pregnant the thought of dragging babes to their doom made him feel sick.

It made him feel monstrous.

"You have lost your touch, kelpie."

Murdoch retreated from the shore into darker, deeper waters before materialising and turning to face the Unseelie witch who had spoken. He expected her to grin her bizarre, twisted grin at him, as she usually did, but the creature appeared uncharacteristically serious.

In her hands was an adult leg – a man's, going by the size of it – which she promptly threw in Murdoch's direction. He snapped and gnashed his teeth at it, devouring every last morsel of flesh and bone in a matter of seconds. The Unseelie watched him do so with gleaming, silver eyes; she nodded in satisfaction when Murdoch finished eating.

"You have been away awhile," she said. "I had a notion you would be hungry."

Murdoch growled softly, though there was no malice behind the sound. "And why would you concern yourself with my appetite, faerie?"

"How often must we attest that we are friends before you trust me?" she asked, visibly affronted.

"Forever," Murdoch replied. And then, with some reluctance: "Regardless, thank you. You are right; I have lost my touch. I cannot bear the thought of devouring a child."

"Understandable, given the circumstances."

Murdoch eyed her suspiciously. "Maybe so. You have no qualms with eating children, I presume."

The faerie merely laughed, insidious and sinister. She swam away from the shore and the children, in the direction of the waterfall pool that connected the loch and the forest, looking behind her every so often to ensure Murdoch was following her. He complied, if only because it was clear the Unseelie either had something she wanted to say or show him.

"What have you learned about the Unseelie Court during your travels?" she asked after a while, genuinely curious. Murdoch recalled that the witch was not supposed to have any contact with faeries – Seelie *or* Unseelie – and that she had to rely on any new information reaching her ears through outlaws, passers-by and unfortunate victims of her insatiable appetite.

Or visions, he mused, thinking of the one the creature had shared with him. Less than six months remained before Sorcha was supposed to become pregnant with Murdoch's child, if he was to believe what the witch had seen, though given Sorcha's current state of imprisonment Murdoch was beginning to seriously doubt the prophecy.

"Eirian has not left his castle since he hid Sorcha within its walls," Murdoch finally replied, voice quiet and insubstantial in the water. "Every creature who isn't a member of his Court that has entered the castle has not been witnessed leaving. That is all I know."

Murdoch wished he had learned more during his scouting mission; alas, it had been difficult enough to find a water nymph who both lived close to the Unseelie Court and had been willing to talk. He could only hope that Lachlan had learned more than the kelpie had during his absence, though Murdoch was not feeling hopeful about this.

"Hmm," the Unseelie witch murmured, carefully traversing the narrow stream that connected the loch to the waterfall pool. When she reached the pool itself she cast a furtive glance all around, then relaxed when it became clear nobody was nearby. She sighed happily. "I have not been so close to the faerie realm in decades, kelpie. And I would not dare to, were you not with me."

"I am glad to be of service, I suppose," Murdoch replied, checking for himself that there truly was nobody around before reverting to his human form. He broke through the surface of the water, shivering in the chilly air beneath the shade of the trees, then hauled himself out of the pool to lie on a patch of grass illuminated by the afternoon sun. His sodden shirt and trousers soon began to dry, and eventually Murdoch began to feel more like a human and less like a monstrous water horse.

"Will you really become mortal for your lass?" the faerie asked after a long stretch of not-unpleasant silence, as if reading his mind.

Murdoch replied almost immediately, with a surety he had never experienced before falling in love with Sorcha. "Yes."

A pause. And then: "I have a way that you can save her from the silver king."

"You – what?!" Murdoch cried, sitting bolt upright to stare at the ugly, wretched creature who was in turn watching him intently. She reached the bank of the pool, rested her head on silver-scaled arms and closed her eyes for slightly too long to have been blinking. When she opened her eyes again her pupils had contracted to pinpricks, leaving naught but mercury in her bulbous eyes.

"Upon a horse with a king and a babe in tow she went, and upon a horse with a king and a babe in tow she can return," the witch said, voice terrifyingly beautiful and seductive just as it had been when she'd voiced her original vision to Murdoch. "Under no other circumstances can you break her promise with the Unseelie king. But recreate such circumstances exactly, and he cannot demand her back."

Murdoch chewed over the witch's words carefully. He had heard of a tale akin to this before – of a mortal man stolen from his true love by a faerie queen, and his love's quest to retrieve him. In truth he'd thought it sounded ridiculous and over-complicated, but that was exactly how the rules of the fae worked.

And, after all, Murdoch was a horse, and Lachlan a king.

Slowly, surely, a giddy grin began to creep across his face, and Murdoch rose to his feet. "This is...I can make that work. Lachlan and I can make that work. I – how can I thank you?" he asked, euphoria filling every corner of his body as the Unseelie witch grinned right back.

She laughed. "Oh, you can thank me in due time. Only do not forget me, when you have your lovely lady back."

"I could live another five hundred years and not forget you," Murdoch replied, not caring when a broken branch prodded the bottom of his shoeless feet. He had always returned to his human form by the Darrow house; this was the first time in a long time he had done so within the confines of the forest. He glanced at the witch. "Though I sincerely hope I do *not* live for another five hundred years."

"A pity," the Unseelie said. "A real pity. Well, you best be off to tell the Seelie king the good news. Best of luck to you, kelpie."

With a final nod Murdoch turned and fled through the forest, darting beneath the trees with a grace he had never before experienced upon two feet. He was impatient to reach the Seelie Court; to regale Lachlan and Ailith with his news.

They could save Sorcha. They were *going* to save Sorcha, and Lachlan's baby, too.

But when Murdoch caught a glimmer of golden skin half an hour later he paused in the midst of his mirthful run, frowning at the figure staggering through the forest just ahead of him. "...fox?" he called. When the faerie in question turned to see who had shouted Murdoch called out again, more confidently this time. But something was wrong.

Lachlan was crying.

Murdoch's very blood froze in his veins. "What is wrong?" he asked, fearful of the answer Lachlan would give. The Seelie king's eyes were red-rimmed and terrible; Murdoch had never seen his face so pale before. "Lachlan, what has happened?"

A few seconds of anguished silence. And then: "T-the baby," Lachlan stuttered. "She lost the baby."

CHAPTER SIXTEEN

Lachlan

"No."

"It is true," Lachlan said, which was a pointless thing to say given that he could not lie. But Murdoch was looking at him as if he had spoken nonsense - as if he could not understand the words Lachlan had uttered.

Lachlan hated that he was crying. He hated even more that, upon realising what he was doing, the tears fell heavier than before and Lachlan with them, collapsing to his knees even though he had an audience consisting of the one creature he never wished to display weakness in front of.

The kelpie's pitch-black eyes grew wide at the sight of him. "What happened, Lachlan?" Murdoch asked, surprising Lachlan by using his actual name for the second time in as many minutes. "How do you - did an envoy finally return?"

Lachlan shook his miserable head. Above him the

sun filtered through the trees, warming his skin and hair even though his very core was frozen. It was as if he was stuck in the cold, unrelenting fog of the Unseelie Court, never to remember what heat felt like again.

"I saw her, kelpie," he finally said. "Ailith had the idea of turning me into a fox so I could sneak into the Unseelie Court unnoticed. And it...it actually worked. I wish we had thought of the idea sooner. I wish..."

"There is no point wishing for anything now, fox," Murdoch said. He sat down upon the forest floor in front of Lachlan, face constructed into something resembling control. But Lachlan could see right through the veneer; Murdoch was inches away from breaking down just as Lachlan had.

Once he told him what Eirian had done to Sorcha, he imagined the kelpie's control would melt away entirely.

Murdoch's expression darkened at Lachlan's foreboding silence. "For the love of the forest speak clearly," he demanded. "I cannot read your mind. What exactly happened? Do not keep secrets from me now!"

"...immortal," Lachlan mumbled, looking away as he spoke. He could not bear to face the kelpie as he acknowledged the Unseelie king's evil act with his own words – his own voice. "Eirian took Sorcha's mortality away, and she – she lost our—"

The sentence ended in a string of incomprehensible sobs. Lachlan did not think he had ever cried so much; he had not believed it *possible* for him to do so. They wracked through his body, bending him double and stabbing at his stomach like knives instead of tears. "O-our child," he stammered, "the magic took the babe away."

It was Murdoch's turn to be silent. Lachlan was vaguely aware of the man's ragged, accelerated breathing, as if the mere action of processing what Lachlan had said was painful. *That is because it is,* he thought, wishing he could turn back into a fox simply so he could claw away at his own stomach. *I have never been in so much pain.*

"...does he know?" Murdoch eventually asked. "The Unseelie king, I mean. Does he know Sorcha lost—"

"There was no time to ask about it," Lachlan replied, his words more a croak than anything else. He gulped, and forced himself to straighten his back against the tree he was sitting by, and when he wiped away the tears from his eyes Lachlan found that he could discuss the topic at hand so long as he dealt with it in as detached a manner as possible.

"But she is alive and well, save for the fact she has lost her appetite," he continued numbly. "I told her she has to keep up her strength, but now...I wonder if she even wants to. Clara never wanted to be immortal."

Murdoch banged a fist against the earth beneath him. A low, rumbling snarl began in the back of his throat – a sound Lachlan had only heard from him in his true form before. It was thoroughly discomfiting to hear such a sound emitted from the mouth of a human.

Except Murdoch was not human, and Lachlan had never been gladder for it.

"He did not break the tenets of Sorcha's promise by making her immortal, did he?" the kelpie asked, still snarling.

Lachlan shook his head. "Everything she agreed to still holds true. Unless Eirian makes a move to end our lives – directly, irrefutably by his hand, that is – he still holds claim over her. But that does not mean we will not get her back. I do not care what it takes to do so."

It was then that Lachlan noticed a despondence in Murdoch's demeanour that, for some reason, he did not think had anything to do with the terrible news he had placed at the creature's feet.

"What is wrong, horse?" he asked, bending forwards an inch as if intending to console Murdoch before thinking better of it. Lachlan frowned. "You were... happy...when you came across me. What had you learned in your travels?"

Murdoch's eyes were far too bright as he stared at his own hands. "It means nothing now."

That only piqued Lachlan's curiosity more. "Tell me."

"I assure you that you do not want to—"

"*Tell me*," Lachlan urged, more insistent this time.

With an air of defeat Murdoch collapsed onto his back to stare up at the late afternoon sky. Lachlan followed his gaze, spying a raven. A normal, natural one, rather than a faerie in disguise. He was tempted to kill the creature anyway.

"Sorcha mentioned my 'Unseelie friend' in Loch Lomond the eve she was taken," Murdoch said, very slowly. "Well, I suppose she actually *is* my friend, all things considered."

Lachlan shifted on the spot, impatient with the speed with which the kelpie was speaking. "Where is this going?" he asked, but Murdoch ignored him.

"She is a witch. A powerful one from days gone by, if she is to be believed. She told me how to save Sorcha, though the information is useless now."

"She...how? How could we save her?"

"I told you; it is useless—"

"For the sake of the forest just tell me, Murdoch!" Lachlan spat, anger beginning to thaw his frozen insides. *Trust the kelpie to rouse me to fury even when I thought I was empty.*

Murdoch cast him a side-long glance. "We have to recreate the circumstances in which Eirian took her away. Upon a horse with a king and a babe in tow, the witch said. Well, between the two of us we have a king and a horse, but a child..."

The weight of Murdoch's words crushed Lachlan as he absorbed them. "We could have...and he would not have been able to take her back?"

"Not without unlawfully spiriting Sorcha away, which would give us cause to wreak havoc to get her back. But if Sorcha has lost your baby then there is nothing we can do."

"So submissive," came a voice from behind them, which was entirely unfamiliar to Lachlan. "And here I was convinced by tales of the fearsome kelpie of Loch Lomond and the wily King of the Seelie. Wizard, you have lied to me."

"I did not," replied a tetchy voice that Lachlan *did* recognise. "It merely seems as if the opponent I've been asked to help defeat is more formidable than anyone I've come across before."

Lachlan could not believe his ears. The kelpie cast his gaze all around him, thoroughly confused, slowly standing up and turning just as Lachlan did the same.

And there, accompanied by a raven-haired man with unnervingly amber eyes, stood the wizard Lachlan had spent years searching for.

The man who had saved his life once upon a time: Julian Thorne.

A mad grin crept across Lachlan's face. "You are late, wizard."

Julian raised an eyebrow. "Going by your current circumstances I would rather say that I'm precisely on time."

CHAPTER SEVENTEEN

Sorcha

Several days had passed since Lachlan's miraculous, impossible visit in the form of a fox. Sorcha was still struggling to wrap her head around what had transpired, though that was partly due to how hungry she was. She had hardly eaten in weeks, her grief and anger and abject, intolerable loss eating away at her, instead. But she knew she had to kick herself out of her stupor. Lachlan and Murdoch would never forgive her if she didn't.

More importantly, Sorcha would never forgive herself.

It was time to do something with the immortal life that had been thrust into her arms.

"Miss Sorcha?" came a placid, feminine voice from the door, interrupting her reverie. For a moment Sorcha was thrown back to the Seelie Court, to Ailith and her soft utterances of the same phrase. But there was no affection to be had in this unfamiliar voice speaking her name.

"Come in," Sorcha sighed, immediately regretting giving the voice permission to enter.

The faerie who opened the door kept her silver eyes level with the mirror upon the wall opposite her, entirely avoiding looking at Sorcha curled up like a ball by the fire. She placed a dress protected in a bag of white linen upon the bed. "King Eirian requires your presence for dinner in his private chambers."

Oh, for the love of the forest, no.

But Sorcha's stomach growled horribly, in direct contradiction to her horror. And she remembered what Eirian had said, the last time he'd deigned to speak or see her. *'Either you clean yourself, feed yourself and get some sleep, or I will do all three for you.'*

Well, I have followed the first, she thought, *since I spend much of my time in the hot springs, but I am guilty of ignoring his second and third rules. If I refuse this meal I have no doubt Eirian will plan something much worse for me.*

"Give me fifteen minutes to ready myself," she told the faerie, who merely nodded and retreated from the room. Sorcha imagined she was likely standing sentry outside the door, and would give her precisely the fifteen minutes Sorcha had asked from her - no more and no less.

It took Sorcha every ounce of willpower she possessed to rise to her feet and stumble over to the bed. With some trepidation she opened the linen bag, expecting the dress within it to be just as insubstantial and otherworldly as the one Eirian had magicked onto her at the Unseelie solstice.

She was therefore surprised to find a simple, knee-length dress of soft ivory, with a delicately embroidered bodice and floating, flouncing skirt. The sleeves were slashed and elbow-length; the neckline sweeping but not nearly as low as the ones Sorcha had seen at the revel.

"I think I actually like this," Sorcha murmured, throwing off her current clothes and sliding into the dress. It fit perfectly, though Sorcha had expected it to. It was likely created *for* her, after all, and faerie tailors had some of the best eyes in the world.

Sorcha moved through to the washroom to splash ice-cold water on her face, then grabbed a soft bristle brush and ran it through her hair until it was free of tangles and tumbled over her shoulders in a far less haphazard fashion that it had done moments earlier. She resisted checking her reflection in the large mirror in her room, for she suspected Eirian used it to keep an eye on her.

After a brief search by the bed Sorcha came to the conclusion that the dress the Unseelie servant had brought in did not come with shoes, though she did not mind going barefoot. Sorcha had become used to the practice with all her time in the Seelie Court and her summers spent close to the shore of Loch Lomond, and had ultimately always misliked having to wear shoes in general.

When she heard a knock on the door Sorcha knew her fifteen minutes were up. With a surreptitious glance at the mirror she left her room, dutifully following the servant as she wound her way down the tower and across the grand, sweeping entrance hall of Eirian's castle.

Do not think of Lachlan and Murdoch, Sorcha thought, steeling her frayed nerves. *Do not think of home at all.* She knew the Unseelie king would work out something was awry if she wasn't careful, though Sorcha's general despondency over the past three weeks would go some ways in masking any odd behaviour she might exhibit after Lachlan's secret visit.

But that very thought caused Sorcha's heart to beat altogether too quickly. *Eirian might well know of Lachlan's visit already,* she panicked, fighting to keep her expression as neutral as possible when the servant glanced back at her. *That could be why he wishes to see me tonight. What will I do if he knows? What will* he *do if he—*

"Sorcha Darrow. Please, have a seat."

Sorcha's eyes widened in surprise when she caught sight of the Unseelie king, resplendent in a deep blue tailcoat and matching trousers, his signature, slashed shirt and silver jewellery flashing from his neck and wrists and fingers.

She fought back a gulp. *I was so lost in my thoughts I did not keep track of how I got here.* But then Sorcha looked around Eirian's chambers and realised she was at the top of a tower opposite the one she'd been imprisoned in, going by the view through the tall, arched window behind Eirian. She shivered, for though it was April and no more fog roiled and tumbled around the castle the Unseelie king's chambers were chilly.

Eirian smiled at her expectantly, sharp teeth gleaming in the silvered candlelight that filled the room. "A seat, Miss Darrow?" he said again, indicating towards a high-backed, velvet-lined chair that sat beside a circular table with impossibly spindly legs. Behind it was a large and frameless mirror that took up much of the wall; for a moment Sorcha wondered what Eirian saw within the glass.

I do not wish to know, she decided, closing the gap between herself and the Unseelie king to sit upon the chair he proffered her in careful silence. He nodded approvingly. Then, with the flick of a wrist adorned with chains and heavy, midnight-blue jewels, he dismissed the servant who had shown Sorcha to his chambers.

"The dress is to your tastes, I see," he said, sitting down opposite Sorcha. It wasn't a question, so Sorcha did not answer. Eirian chuckled. "Silence does not become you. You are enjoying the hot springs, I trust? My servants tell me you spend much of your time—"

"Is anything on the table made of faerie food?" Sorcha asked, cutting Eirian's musings short to ask the one question she absolutely needed a truthful answer to. The food and drink presented before her was beautiful, ranging from savoury, rosemary-scented pies to delicate sugared plums to deep, sweet berry wine. Sorcha's stomach clawed at her to reach for the nearest morsel and stuff it in her mouth.

But something grew in Eirian's unnatural eyes in response to her question – a sharpness, perhaps – that Sorcha did not like. His lips fell into a hard line, and he cocked his head to the side to regard her. Sorcha found that she could not maintain eye contact, so she focused on the way Eirian's long, silken hair fell across his shoulder, instead.

"No," Eirian eventually said. "Everything here is safe for you to eat and drink...unless you asked the question with the intention of consuming faerie food?"

Sorcha deigned not to answer the question, for her answer was obvious. Without waiting for Eirian to say anything else, and for fear that he could somehow read in her mannerisms that something was wrong, Sorcha nimbly chose one of the pies sitting on a plate in front of her and began to eat it.

She was painfully aware of Eirian's inscrutable gaze upon her as she ate, even when he finally picked up his knife and fork and began to dine, too. It was in this way that Sorcha had perhaps the most awkward meal of her life, though the food was just as delicious as the food in the Seelie Court – if not more so.

I would never admit that, though, she mused. *Lachlan would be furious if I said such a thing.*

"You are smiling."

Sorcha froze, for the very thought of Lachlan had indeed caused the hint of a smile to cross her face. "The food here is wonderful," she said, relieved to find the half-truth dripping off her tongue in an instant.

Eirian seemed pleased by her answer. He leaned back in his chair, a satisfied look on his face. "You would have learned this earlier, had you deigned to try it."

"I think I had as good a reason as any to have lost my appetite."

That sharpness again. Sorcha forced herself to face it this time, though Eirian's gaze made her deeply uncomfortable. But the Unseelie king's next question caught her by surprise in its gentleness. "How are you faring?" he asked. "It is good to see some colour return to your cheeks."

"I...so long as I do not think much about anything I am faring as well as one might expect."

When the Unseelie king laughed Sorcha's cheeks burned. There was something about having him laugh at her that left Sorcha feeling distinctly humiliated.

"You have a clever tongue, Miss Darrow," Eirian said, taking a long draught of wine without once tearing his silver eyes away from hers. "It is hard to believe you were not always a faerie."

"I am not one now, either."

"You are in all but name, now that you are immortal."

Sorcha bit back a retort. Eirian was baiting her, it seemed, and she was far too easily falling into his trap. *If I am not careful I will let something slip about Lachlan, and all will be lost.*

"You have not once asked for information about the Seelie Court, and your bereft suitors," Eirian said, very softly, though the words hit Sorcha's ears as if he had shouted them.

"You would not tell me anything if I asked...unless to torment me," Sorcha replied, choosing every word as carefully as if she were picking her way across a precipitous mountainside. "I am not wrong, am I?"

Eirian waved a dismissive hand, bracelets and bangles jingling musically as he did so. "Most likely. But you are taking the fun out of this for me, Sorcha. Won't you play the begging, desperate prisoner for me even a little?"

"I do not think so," Sorcha replied, flinching despite herself at Eirian's solitary use of her first name. "But you must have known I wouldn't."

"I am beginning to understand that, yes. You are an interesting creature."

She shook her head. "Not so. I am but a lowly

mort-"

When Eirian cackled at Sorcha's half-sentence she looked down at her hands, immediately on the verge of tears. She had spoken the truth, when she told the Unseelie king she was faring well enough so long as she did not think about anything. But the moment Sorcha dallied with the idea of immortality...

"I have had my fill," she said, not quite succeeding in smoothing a crack from her voice. "May I be excused?"

The look Eirian gave her suggested he hadn't nearly had *his* fill, though he nodded his head. "You may go. But you will return her at the same time in three days. And three days after that, and three days after that, until I see fit to end the arrangement."

Sorcha said nothing. There was nothing she *could* say to get out of such an arrangement, if Eirian himself wished it, and she knew he could easily make it every night instead if he so desired. Without another glance at the Unseelie king she fled his chambers, somehow not surprised in the slightest to find the faerie who had led her there waiting by the door.

"Take me back," she said, allowing the servant to walk ahead of her to lead her to her room.

Forever only grows longer, she thought, morose, when she collapsed beside the fireplace despite the fact her pristine dress became covered in soot within seconds. *Dinner with Eirian every three nights will be torture.*

It did not escape Sorcha that this was most likely exactly what the silver king had intended.

CHAPTER EIGHTEEN

Lachlan

"Your home truly is beautiful, Lachlan of the Seelies."

"It would have been more beautiful with Clara in it, had you shown up when I started looking for you," Lachlan countered as he led the way back to the palace, nerves still too raw from his meeting with Sorcha and Murdoch's devastating news to temper his words.

The wizard's amber-eyed companion snorted. "I think I like you, Seelie king."

"Who is this man, Julian?"

"I second that," Murdoch chimed in, "though it seems as if both of these men know about me already."

Julian Thorne cast his gaze over Murdoch, a small smile on his face. There were a few new lines creasing the skin around his eyes, and there was a hint of grey at the sides of his temples, but all in all Lachlan figured the past seven years had been good to the wizard.

"Of course I have heard of you," Julian told

Murdoch. "You are the reason the Seelie king was in dire need of my help all those years ago."

"And is, of course, still in your debt, I would imagine," the raven-haired man added on. He brought a shard of tourmaline out of his pocket, held it up to the dying afternoon light and inspected it with a frown upon his face. "Wizard, this really did take us right into the centre of the Seelie Court. You were not lying when you told me it came from here."

Julian rolled his eyes. "Why would I lie to you?"

"To impress Red, of course."

"How many times do I have to—"

"*Who are you?*" both Murdoch and Lachlan insisted, exchanging an exasperated look that Lachlan had often seen Ailith and Sorcha share when witnessing him and the kelpie arguing with one another. His heart twisted at the thought of Sorcha; going by the momentary wince that crossed Murdoch's face Lachlan could only imagine a similar thought had crossed his mind, too.

Julian's companion bowed gracefully in response. "My apologies. The wizard always brings out the worst in me, you see. We aren't exactly what one would call *friends,* though our better halves decidedly are." When he came out of his bow Lachlan got a closer look at the man, and though he seemed to be at a similar stage of his life as Julian himself there was something ageless about him, too.

It is his eyes, Lachlan thought. *They are not human, somehow.*

The man caught Lachlan staring, and he smiled an animalistic grin that was somehow familiar to him. "My name is Adrian Wolfe," he said, "and I am arrogant enough to believe that you would most sincerely regret using my full name against me, faerie."

Something about Adrian's manner irked Lachlan, though he assumed that was the point. To his left Murdoch was appraising the man with a critical eye and a familiar, intimidating silence. Lachlan found himself appreciating the kelpie's presence, for the creature was able to look through deceptions just as well as he was – if not more.

Lachlan took a step towards Julian. "If the two of you are not friends, as Mr Wolfe so cannily described, then why is he here?"

"He has skills that near no-one else has," the wizard explained, though it seemed to physically pain him to admit it. He glowered in Adrian's direction, though the man deliberately ignored him. He prowled around Murdoch, instead, examining him with the same curiosity the kelpie was showing him.

Lachlan frowned. "Please elaborate."

"Curses," Adrian replied, still circling Murdoch. "The weaving of words. Blood magic. The wizard's strength lies in the physicality of magic – of fire and flesh and gold. My own expertise is far more like your own, faerie, although without the caveat that I must not lie."

A shiver ran through Lachlan despite himself, though it was tinged with excitement. Adrian Wolfe was powerful, of that he had no doubt. That he was on the side of the Seelie Court was an advantage Lachlan could only have hoped for.

If he's on our side, that is.

"Name your price," Lachlan said, bringing everyone's attention back to him. Even Murdoch stopped watching

Adrian, an uncertain look upon his face.

"Careful what you promise, fox," he said. "You are not in a position to—"

"I know what I am and am not currently in a position to promise," Lachlan cut in. He turned to Julian. "The Seelie are in panic mode right now. King Eirian's presence looms over us; everyone knows that we are likely not strong enough to defeat our southron brethren. But if we can gain an advantage over him - if we can defeat him - there is not a thing in the world I would not promise you."

Julian's face paled. "What has he done to you, Lachlan? All the news I received was that you required my assistance to take him down, but no reason as to why."

"He took Sorcha."

It was Murdoch who answered. The way he spoke - the way he *looked* as he spoke - was all both Julian and Adrian needed to fully understand what was going on.

Julian nodded. "For saving your life seven years ago and helping you now - that makes two favours you owe me. I ask, for the first, that myself and anyone I would consider family will always be safe and welcome within your side of the faerie realm, and may find room at your table in the Seelie Court."

"Done. And the second?"

"The second I would leave for Evie," he said, smiling. "She would never forgive me if I took a faerie's favour from her. When your war is fought, Seelie king, I would ask that you grant her whatever she wishes."

Lachlan was starkly reminded of why he had put his trust in Julian in the first place. The relationship he'd had with his golden-haired love was something so rare and pure that he'd instinctively known the pair would do anything for each other.

"Gladly done," he said. "And you, Mr Wolfe? What would you have of me?"

When the man did not answer immediately Lachlan knew he would not like what he eventually said. Adrian ran a hand through his hair, rearranging a solitary streak of white that broke the black in the process. "I have no need of a favour at present," he said, smiling softly. "And, indeed, it seems as if your current problem may take months to solve, given the tricky political position you're in. I would rather have the notion of a favour looming over you, Seelie king. And you, too, kelpie."

Murdoch's eyes glowered like coals. "Your skill set had best be worth such a thing."

"Oh, trust me," Adrian said, "it is. I will prove most useful – on the battlefield as well as off it."

"Then a favour in the future is granted," Lachlan said, "though I am curious as to what you mean by *on the battlefield.*"

When Adrian grinned again Lachlan realised why it was so familiar. *Like mine,* he thought. *Vulpine. No... lupine.*

"They do not call me Mr Wolfe for nothing, Seelie king," he said, amber eyes glittering in amusement. He drew back his top lip, introducing a snarl to his smile. "Now, let's get planning."

CHAPTER NINETEEN

Eirian

For three months now King Eirian had been dealing with silence on two very different fronts.

The first was the Seelie Court. After Sorcha had initially been spirited away the entire realm had been pandemonium. There was hardly a corner one could visit without news of Eirian's deal with the Seelie king's paramour. Lachlan had sent envoy after envoy to collect information. Numerous performers and gossip-mongers sought an audience in the Unseelie Court in order to be the first ones to know just what exactly was going on. Eirian had prevented them all from leaving, of course, but he had not expected the Seelies to stop trying to fish for information.

Except that they did. Now that Sorcha had been locked away in the Unseelie castle for thirteen weeks straight the Seelie Court was a wall of silence. Eirian had no way of knowing what they were planning, for in an ironic twist of fate any envoys *he* sent to his northern brethren did not return.

Any Unseelie living beneath the surface of lakes and rivers and lochs were keeping quiet about the wanderings of the kelpie, too, out of sheer terror. Eirian misliked how much independent power he had. The monster was not bound by any of the laws of faerie; if he had an impulse to attack the Unseelie Court Eirian had no doubt that he could indulge it.

Keeping hold of Sorcha Darrow was supposed to keep Lachlan and the water horse under my thumb, he mused. *It feels like they are planning something.*

Eirian almost laughed at the notion. Of course they were planning something, but he doubted very much that it would work. Both the golden king and the kelpie would stay their hand the moment Eirian threatened Sorcha, and that was ultimately all the leverage he needed to keep them in their place. *Let them scheme and sit in silence. It will all be for naught.*

All he needed was a little more time. Another few years and Eirian would bring down a full-fledged assault against the Seelie Court, and take control of the entire realm. He only wished that he was not quite so alone in the venture, for though it had been Eirian's plan all along to be rid of his half-brother and his nephew, now that they had been gone seven years the Unseelie king had to admit that there was a part of him that almost missed his family.

Almost.

The second wall of silence Eirian had to deal with was, of course, Sorcha Darrow.

The former mortal was certainly proving to be a formidable opponent. Even now, as she sat opposite him for their three-nightly dinner arrangements, looking perfectly lovely and innocent in a periwinkle dress of gossamer and spider-silk, Sorcha had refused to respond to any of Eirian's questions and comments for the best part of an hour. She answered only as and when she decided it prudent.

Her behaviour had long since grated on the Unseelie king's nerves.

Sorcha proved immune to Eirian granting her the freedom to roam the castle, and insisting that she be left alone in the hot springs if she wished to enjoy them by herself, and the dresses, jewellery and pretty silver combs he gifted her every week. Sorcha did not care that her captor was doing everything to make her comfortable. It did not make her fonder of the place. It did not make her rage and scream in frustration. It did not make her cry, or outwardly appear to miss her family.

No, it simply did nothing at all.

It therefore stood to reason that the Unseelie king had constructed a new plan of attack...and intended to put it into action that very night.

"You cannot stay silent forever, little bird," he told Sorcha, refilling their wine glasses as he did so. "I can tell how much you are dying to speak and sing and scream."

Sorcha eyed the wine carefully. Every evening the two of them dined together she asked the same question: *is any of the meal made using faerie food?* Every time Eirian had truthfully answered no, and tonight was no different. So Sorcha, after a moment of hesitation, took her glass when Eirian finished refilling it and took a long draught from the golden wine. Seelie summer wine, since it was June, and Eirian felt very much like indulging Sorcha's tastes before setting his plan in motion.

"I am not a bird," Sorcha muttered, a moment or two later.

Eirian almost smiled. "And yet I've heard tell you sing like one, over and over again, though I have yet to hear you myself."

"And you won't." A pause. And then: "Why do you care so much about that, anyway?"

"Why, Miss Darrow, are you asking *me* a question?" Eirian said, holding a hand over his heart in mock surprise.

Sorcha clicked her tongue in disgust. "It does not matter."

"Oh, but it does. You are curious. I knew you must be. I have been asking you to sing for five years now, after all."

When she did not reply Eirian sighed. Sorcha's mismatched eyes glimmered in the dim light of his chambers, one green flame and one blue. He was fond of her eyes, in the way a magpie loved shiny objects. He had no doubt Lachlan and the kelpie were both equally as enamoured with them.

"I imagine you are well aware of how covetous my kind can be," Eirian said, deciding to give Sorcha an answer to her question instead of teasing her. Her eyes widened; Eirian saw her barely suppress a gulp of interest. *She is far more curious than she would have me know,* he thought. *That is good.*

"When we hear of mortals with great skills," he continued, "we doubtlessly want them. We find any way to bring that individual's gifts within our power –

compliment them, promise them the world, charm them to join the faerie realm...or use their name to enchant them, if they prove to be resistant." Eirian gave Sorcha a look loaded with meaning, then, though she did not flinch away. There was something in her expression that screamed *you wouldn't dare.*

It was not as if Eirian did not *dare* use Sorcha's name to enchant her, though in truth the Unseelie king did not yet know her full name. It was, rather, that he did not want to. He wanted her as lucid and aware of everything that happened to her as possible, for all the years to come.

A night or two in oblivion, however...

"I do not believe it is as simple as you merely wanting my voice just to have it," Sorcha replied, certain.

Eirian grinned. "You would be correct. I want it because the creatures who love you cherish it. I told you; faeries are covetous creatures. And if it is our neighbour – our rival and enemy – who has something pretty...well, then we want it even more."

"You are so *petty,*" Sorcha replied, indignant enough to forget her rule of silence. She rose from the table, moving over to the fireplace with a sweep of her delicate, feather-light dress. The flames danced in the hearth, painting Sorcha's skin the colour of sunset. "Your entire kind. Petty to a fault."

"You say this as if humans are any better."

"Humans have perhaps eighty years at best to live; it is no wonder they want everything they can reach. Faeries...you have forever."

It was interesting to hear Sorcha talk about humans as if they were a species entirely separate from her. That she did the same for faeries caused Eirian to wonder just how confused she was about what her place in the world now was.

Never far from me, he thought. *That is her place in the world, so long as she holds value.*

"You are taking this too personally," Eirian said, standing up to join Sorcha by the fireplace. He took with him a bowl of sugared plums, which he had learned were her favourite the very first day he met her, in London, when she had gazed at the confections in the window of a baker's shop and realised that the glimmers reflected on the glass were not what they appeared to be.

"And how else am I supposed to take it?" she demanded. "You wish to hear me sing so you can possess my voice, simply to win another victory against Lachlan. That seems rather personal to me."

Eirian popped a sugared plum in his mouth in response, which only irritated Sorcha further. She snarled at the fire, entirely avoiding the Unseelie king's gaze, though grabbed a plum from the bowl he was holding and bit into it with a viciousness Eirian relished.

"I suppose it should make me happy," Sorcha mused, more to herself than to Eirian. "To know that you wish to hear me sing and never will, I mean."

Her lovely hair flashed copper in the firelight, in stark contrast to the blues and purples and silvers of Eirian's chambers. There was something poetic about it; the Unseelie king thought he might have written a song about it, once upon a time.

Another time, long, long ago.

Eirian cocked his head to one side. "You forget that the reason your fox – and your kelpie – adore your voice so much is that it is something truly special."

"And that should matter to me because...?" Sorcha wondered, blithely eating another plum as Eirian gleefully watched her pupils begin to dilate and her movements become slower and slower.

"Because it means *you* are special, even without their attentions," Eirian said, placing the bowl in his hands onto the mantelpiece above the fire to help steady Sorcha when she stumbled. "Which means I wish dearly to hear you sing, simply for myself. You were correct; this *is* personal. Are you feeling quite all right, Sorcha Darrow?"

She was staring at him, bleary-eyed and confused. Sorcha's cheeks had flushed, though she began to rub her arms as if she were freezing. "What have you...what is wrong with me?" she asked, following Eirian's gaze to the sugared plums with some difficulty. "No...no. You have not—"

"Never turn your back on a meal prepared by a faerie," he said, voice dripping with deliberate danger and seduction fully intended to entrap Sorcha in his grasp. "You might just find he has offered you something you really should not eat."

CHAPTER TWENTY

Sorcha

Sorcha Darrow was dizzy. Sorcha Darrow was confused. Sorcha Darrow could barely see.

Sorcha Darrow did not care.

"So this is faerie fruit," she said, altogether far too happily considering what had just happened to her. There was a part of her brain that was telling her this was wrong, that she had been poisoned, but that part was diminishing by the minute. "I have never..."

"Never?" came a voice Sorcha vaguely recognised as King Eirian. But all the animosity – all the fear and anger and sorrow - that she'd felt towards the faerie mere moments ago had disappeared. His voice affected her differently now. It was inviting. Flirtatious.

Dangerous.

Sorcha always longed for dangerous.

"Never," she repeated, shaking her head in an

exaggerated fashion. "I did not wish to lose myself." She flounced from the fireplace to the gargantuan mirror in Eirian's chambers, trying her best to focus on her own reflection with little success. She could make out her wavy, dark auburn hair, and the pretty colour of her floor-length, floaty dress, but that was it. Whenever she tried to zone in on her face it hurt her head, so Sorcha stopped trying.

But when the Unseelie king crossed the stone floor to stand beside her Sorcha could see every detail of his form in the mirror.

His almost translucent white shirt, billowing in some non-existent breeze and begging Sorcha to follow the deep slash in the material all the way down to the faerie's navel.

His skin, which was silver in one light, blue in the next, then back to silver in the space of a blink.

His mercurial eyes and predatory grin, complete with razor teeth that could easily tear out Sorcha's throat.

His long, pointed ears and the jewels that adorned them, reminding Sorcha for a moment of the beautiful silver earring Lachlan had once owned.

The one I broke, to free him.

"You do not lose yourself," Eirian said, voice soft upon the air between them. He reached a hand out to the mirror, so Sorcha did the same. The glass was cold and solid beneath her fingertips, which surprised her; Sorcha had expected that she might fall through the surface. "Faerie fruit merely lowers your inhibitions. Allows you to indulge urges you might otherwise be too cautious to enjoy."

Sorcha considered this for a moment, then

discovered her brain was too heavy to understand such a complicated explanation. "Where does the mirror go?" she asked, instead.

Eirian chuckled. The sound was pleasantly musical to Sorcha's ears, and she longed to hear more of it. "Wherever I want...within reason. I cannot reach the Seelie Court through it, for example. But I could reach a winding London street, or an ostentatious art exhibit."

"You,.." Sorcha shook her head, then smiled at some notion she could scarcely comprehend but that made her happy nonetheless. "Lachlan is strong enough to keep you out."

If she had been in her right mind Sorcha would have seen Eirian bristle at such a comment. Instead, all she saw was the easy smile of his reflection, and the way the Unseelie king inched closer towards her.

"Your fox would not make a very good king if he was not strong," Eirian said. Sorcha nodded her enthusiastic agreement.

"He is stronger than he thinks, I believe. Nobody would follow him if he were not."

"So you trust in his strength?"

"Absolutely," Sorcha replied, moving over to the solitary, curved window in Eirian's chambers as if she were floating. It was open; she revelled in the cool night air upon her skin as she stared out at the inky sky, wondering how close the summer solstice was. *Have I really been here over three months?* she wondered. *Has it been so long?*

Eirian did not move to join her at first. Sorcha vaguely heard him pacing to and fro across the stone floor, footsteps muffled whenever he reached one of his finely-woven rugs.

"So who is stronger?" the Unseelie king asked, after a moment of silence that could well have lasted hours and hours.

Sorcha turned her head to blink at him. "Who is stronger than whom?"

"Your fox, or the kelpie?"

It was not a question anybody had ever asked Sorcha. In her usual, lucid state it was not a question she would have ever answered. "Murdoch," she said, without an ounce of doubt and a generous measure of pride. "My kelpie is stronger than most any of the fair folk."

"So if Lachlan ever meant you harm," Eirian began, taking another step or two towards Sorcha, "what would your kelpie do?"

"He would drown him whilst he was sleeping," Sorcha replied, matter-of-factly. "But Murdoch would never do that."

A pause. "And why not?"

"Because Lachlan would never mean me harm."

"So you trust the two of them, alone, without you?"

Here was another answer Sorcha had no doubt about. An angelic smile crossed her face as she thought of her dark kelpie and her golden fox. "More than anything."

Again, had Sorcha been in her right mind she would have seen the flash of irritation that crossed Eirian's face. But he hid it behind another heartbreakingly beautiful smile, and when he reached the window and slid his arms around Sorcha's waist she did not pull away.

"You are lucky to be so loved, Miss Darrow," he

said, leaning his chin upon her left shoulder. Sorcha's heart was already beating too quickly; something inside her told her that if she turned around to face the Unseelie king it would beat all the faster. So she kept her eyes locked on the stars in the uncharacteristically clear night sky, though part of her wondered why the sky was so dark and haunting when it was already midsummer.

She did not respond to Eirian's statement so, after an insurmountable amount of silence, he asked, "Why are you so focused on the stars?"

"You are made of starlight," Sorcha replied. "Starlight and dark, empty nothingness."

Eirian chuckled against her ear, tickling her skin. "You flatter me," he said. "Would you like to see the real stars closer than you ever have before, Sorcha?"

But before she could respond Eirian tightened his arms around her waist and vaulted the two of them out of the open window. Sorcha let out a yell, terrified, yet in the space of a second it turned into a cry of delight when it became apparent that she was not falling to her death.

She craned her neck to see Eirian behind her, but he merely grinned. With the slightest of tilts of his head they careened up and up and up, until the air grew thin and Sorcha breathless with it.

"How are you..." she began, but Sorcha could not finish the question. For in the nighttime air Sorcha's skin was as silver as the king who carried her through the sky. She matched the stars clustered all around her, larger than she had ever seen them before as they twinkled their hellos. The moon hung fat and heavy just out of reach; the prized jewel in a decadent crown.

It was perhaps the most magical sight Sorcha had ever witnessed.

Though she couldn't see them, Sorcha could hear the beating of impossibly large wings. Once or twice, out of the corner of her eye, she could have sworn she saw a raven's feather, iridescent in the moonlight, but when she tried to focus on it the feather disappeared.

Sorcha could not truly process what she could see and hear and smell and feel as she was wound through the sky. She was aware of Eirian's arms around her waist, ensuring she did not fall, and the rush of air against her face, but everything else that assaulted her senses felt like a dream.

Another life. Another world.

Before she had the opportunity to breathe again, the two of them were back in Eirian's chambers.

The Unseelie king tugged at his shirt, pulling it over his head and dropping it to the floor before shaking out his hair. Sorcha had only ever seen it immaculate and straight; now it was wild and windswept.

She liked it far better this way.

"Your hair," she said, giggling as she stumbled towards him. "It is as much a mess as mine usually is."

His lips quirked into a smile. "And yet, somehow, you like that. Why is that, Sorcha Darrow?"

"Rules are for accountants. Rules are for lawyers. Rules are for—"

"Anyone but you?"

Sorcha stared at him, wide-eyed and full of adrenaline. "Yes," she answered simply. "They are for ordinary humans."

The Unseelie king closed the gap between them, stroking the length of Sorcha's jawline as her breathing hitched in response. "And you are not one of them."

Eirian's cruel lips found hers, and she did not pull away. For though the kiss was wrong – terribly, monstrously wrong – in her current state of mind Sorcha thought that it was just right.

Then the Unseelie king slowly but surely slid her dress from her shoulders to join his shirt on the cold, stone floor, and the night was lost to gasps and sighs and whispers.

In the light of day those whispers were as sinister as curses. Beneath a moonlit sky they were endless adulations of love.

Sorcha eagerly drank up every last word of them.

CHAPTER TWENTY-ONE

Sorcha

Almost a full nine months had passed before Sorcha was truly aware of it, and the winter solstice was looming on the horizon. She wondered if her grasp of time had changed the moment Eirian stripped her of her mortality.

If it had, she truly wanted nothing more to do with it.

To be numb to so much of my life is horrible, she thought, *though I have to wonder if this is how all otherwordly creatures feel.*

Sorcha did not want to dwell upon this, for if it were true then that meant Lachlan, Murdoch, Ailith and even Ronan and the rest of the Seelie Court always felt this disconnected. It was not something she would wish upon anyone.

A spasm ran through her stomach, bending Sorcha double. She had been plagued by aches and nausea for a few weeks now, though she had hidden her discomfort as best she could from Eirian and the servants he sent to spy on her. Sorcha had been very, very careful to avoid the mirror in her room whenever she felt ill, for the last thing she wanted was for the Unseelie king to gain more leverage against her.

"Why do I feel like this?" she groaned, clutching at her stomach. Sorcha contemplated going to the washroom to vomit, or to the hot springs to soak her aching skin in bubbling, restorative water, but ultimately she did not have the energy to move.

Sorcha wished she knew why she felt the way she did. But she had experienced several odd, prolonged bouts of memory loss that she could not explain over the past half a year, and she was scared to address them. With the way time had affected her since she was spirited away to the Unseelie realm Sorcha would not have been surprised if the gaps in her memory were simply to do with her becoming adjusted to immortality.

Something told her this wasn't the answer.

Every three nights she had dinner with the Unseelie king. On the third of each of these three nights she could never remember what she got up to after their shared meal, no matter how hard she tried. Sorcha shuddered merely thinking about what was going on.

She entirely lacked the courage to confront King Eirian about what he might be doing.

Whenever she thought of such unpleasant subjects Sorcha, as if in defence, forced herself to think of Lachlan or Murdoch or lazy days spent braiding Ailith's impossibly long hair as they traded gossip about Darach and the Seelie Court. *They will work out what to do,* she reassured herself, over and over again. *Eirian was not supposed to make me immortal. Though it doesn't void the promise I made to him it most certainly* changes *things. Nobody who cares about me will let this lie.*

She hoped.

"Mama," Sorcha groaned, when another dagger drove itself into her stomach. As a child she had never been that close to her mother, and as a teenager even less so. Sorcha's initial adventure with Lachan had been what changed her attitude towards the woman who birthed her, despite their differences. Sorcha missed her greatly; all she wanted to do was become a little girl again and cry in her mother's arms, her reassuring hands stroking her daughter's hair.

But Sorcha could not have that, nor could she have a fireside story from her father.

Sorcha Darrow had no family left.

When she heard a knock upon her door Sorcha became rigid, then fled to the washroom in a fit of sudden, inevitable nausea. She did not give the knocker permission to enter - she did not tell them to do anything at all - so when Sorcha heard the heavy door open and shut she knew the faerie who knocked could only be one, specific creature she absolutely did not wish to see.

King Eirian.

"Where are you, Miss Darrow?" Eirian called, voice almost sing-song. Sorcha wished nothing more than to hide in the washroom, out of his sight, until the Unseelie king finally gave up and disappeared.

She knew that would never happen.

"I am - wait just a moment," she gasped, before losing the battle with her stomach to keep what little that was inside it *inside it.* Sorcha heaved, and retched, and by the time she was finished the Unseelie king stood in the doorway to the washroom, watching her with a frown on his face.

He almost looked concerned.

"You are not well," he said.

"C-clearly," Sorcha replied, wiping her mouth with the back of a shaking hand before slowly moving to the nearby basin to splash ice water over her face. It tingled so much that it burned, but Sorcha relished the feeling.

Eirian handed Sorcha a towel for her to dry herself. For a moment she considered not taking it, though she found that she did not have the energy to defy such a harmless gesture. "How long have you been ill?" Eirian asked as she dried her face. "I have not noticed—"

"I have been hiding it," Sorcha told him, barely managing to get to her feet to stumble past the Unseelie king. She made a beeline for her bed but then, in a sudden change of heart, collapsed by the fireplace instead.

Eirian seemed inordinately impressed by her statement, which confused Sorcha to no end. "You truly are a stubborn one, Miss Darrow."

She did not care about what he meant. "What was it that you wanted?" she asked, breathing in the smell of burning wood from the fireplace and sighing in relief when she realised it settled her nausea.

"To see how you are, of course."

"How generous of you."

Sorcha thought Eirian was going to laugh at her reply; instead, he crouched low beside her, a look of unmistakable concern upon his face. "How long have you been ill?" he asked, brushing a hand across Sorcha's forehead. She did not bother pushing it away.

"A few weeks. Do you know why I'm feeling like this?"

Silence. Sorcha watched as Eirian struggled with how to answer her question using some form of the truth, which did not bode well for her at all. "Perhaps," he finally said, and then: "Do not make a sound for a minute."

"What do you—"

He placed a finger to her lips. She resisted the urge to bite it as a warning for him to leave her alone. But Sorcha was deathly curious about what the Unseelie king thought might be wrong with her, so she indulged his request to stay silent.

When his mercurial eyes widened there was something akin to disbelief within them. "That hardly seems possible..." he mumbled. Then, before Sorcha could stop him, Eirian bent his head low and placed an ear against her stomach. She pushed at his shoulders to try and get rid of him but the faerie was far too strong for her shoves to make any impact.

"What are you *doing*?" she demanded. Bile was beginning to rise in her throat again; if Eirian did not move soon Sorcha was sure she would be sick all over his silken hair.

Then perhaps he should not move, she thought, grimly satisfied with the notion of doing something so disgusting to her captor.

"You are pregnant."

Oh.

For a moment Sorcha could not breathe. Could not think. It took every ounce of strength she had in her to process what the Unseelie king had just said to her.

"I cannot be—"

"You are *pregnant,*" Eirian repeated, so obviously delighted that Sorcha was taken entirely aback. The faerie got to his feet, pulling Sorcha along with him. He squeezed her hands so tightly she winced. "For something to happen to the same woman for *two* kings is...impossible. Improbable, at the very least. Some witch or ghoul or seer must have foreseen this. Why have I heard no news of it before? I must search for—"

"How?" Sorcha asked, cutting through Eirian's self-possessed ramblings as she forcefully pulled her hands away from his. "How am I pregnant with..."

Then the Unseelie king's words truly set in. *Two kings, he said. One was Lachlan. The other...*

"No," she gasped, beyond horrified, but when Sorcha tried to take a step away from him Eirian merely grabbed both her wrists in a vice-like grip.

His eyes shone with an excitement she had never seen before. "This changes everything, little bird," he said. "It seems it is time I expedite my plans."

Sorcha did not want to know what those plans were. Going by Eirian's face, however, she had a fairly good – and awful - idea about what he was intending.

"I am afraid I shall have to rearrange tonight's dinner plans, *my love,*" he said, enunciating the final two words with sick and frightful glee. He broke away from Sorcha, quickly making his way to the door before she had a chance to breathe.

He flashed a grin at her. "I have a war to start, you see."

Sorcha did not make it to the washroom in time to vomit once more.

CHAPTER TWENTY-TWO

Lachlan

A rumbling filled the air. Lachlan was startled from his morning doze, shivering back into consciousness in response to the sounds.

"Just what is going on?" he wondered aloud wincing at the weak morning light that hit his eyes when he opened them.

Then Ronan crashed through the doors to Lachlan's chambers, ruddy-faced and panicked. "He is here."

Lachlan frowned. "Who is here?"

"The Unseelie king," the faerie replied, falling over the words in his urgency to utter them. "He is here with an army. He is here to attack us!"

Lachlan leapt to his feet, tense and deathly alert. "He was never supposed to attack us. Not now – not for years, even! I thought no information had leaked out about our planned ambush. So how—"

"I do not know," Ronan cut in, giving Lachlan just enough time to pull on a pair of leather trousers, a shirt, a green-and-gold overcoat and knee-high boots before corralling him out of his chambers towards the strategy room. They met Murdoch on their way there; deep shadows lurked beneath his eyes, making the kelpie look entirely haunted.

"There is a disturbance," he said as they rushed through the door. Ronan cleared the large, central table until all that remained was a detailed map of the Seelie Court and the surrounding forest. "I felt it in the air. What is going on?"

"Eirian," Lachlan muttered. "He is here...with an army. How large, Ronan?"

The horned faerie frowned for a moment. "Scouts say several hundred, but I'm inclined to believe that may be a glamour. If Eirian is leading the army himself I'd say the number is fewer than a hundred...but all well-trained, vicious creatures which are happy to do anything to fulfil their king's desires."

Lachlan considered this for a long moment, just as Julian and Adrian rushed through the door. Julian looked haggard, as if he had been unhappy to find himself roused from sleep; Adrian, on the other hand, looked as if he had been up for hours.

"I guess our winter solstice ambush is no longer happening," the amber-eyed man said, stating the obvious. "So what's the plan?"

Lachlan glanced at the map, thinking hard. It had not rained or snowed for days. The forest was dry and brittle.

If they could catch Eirian's army before they reached the central part of the Seelie Court then they could well defeat him.

After all, the silver king had no idea his opponent had the best fire wizard in Europe on his side.

"Burn them," he said, staring at Julian as his mouth widened into a humourless grin. Out of the corner of his eye he saw Murdoch share a similar reaction, though Adrian looked somewhat hesitant. "Do you have an issue with this?" Lachlan asked the man.

He shook his head. "It is a fine plan – and the best we could hope for on such short notice. I simply have... bad memories...of fire."

"I can keep the fire under control," Murdoch chimed in. "That was supposed to be the plan for the ambush of the revel, anyway, to distract the Unseelie. Burn and drown. Only on a much smaller, less noticeable scale. But I can handle a large fire."

Julian glanced at him. "It could very easily grow out of control in a dry forest like this. Are you sure?"

"Positive."

"Then let's do it." Lachlan indicated towards the entrance of the palace. "Ronan, we need soldiers at every entrance. Guard the revel clearing as best you can, though if you have to choose between the two then prioritise the palace. But keep a small number of soldiers within the underground passages to the clearing, just to keep them protected. Is Ailith awake yet?"

"Being woken as we speak. I've requested she organise the healers."

"Good. Now go."

Ronan nodded, then silently left the room to organise his troops. Lachlan watched as Julian cracked his knuckles, one at a time, and Adrian stretched his back in a slow series of pops.

The two men stared at him. "Better to limber up now than in the field," Adrian said, explaining what they were doing. "Can't be stiff when performing magic."

"I admit to being curious as to just how *wolfish* you are in battle," Lachlan replied.

The man laughed. "I am just as curious to see the kelpie in action."

"Good thing Eirian has brought the fight to us, then," Murdoch said, before moving towards the door. He glanced back over his shoulder, lingering his gaze on Lachlan. "Will this work?"

"It must. It has to."

"Then let's do what we must, because we have to."

As the four of them rushed out of the palace and entered the bitterly cold, dimly lit forest, Lachlan could not help thinking how bizarre the creatures around him were. *Two mortals with magic and a kelpie, of all things. But I would not be strong enough without them. I would be destroyed without them.*

Lachlan did not know if the notion was a good one or not, though he did not have time to dwell upon it. For now he had to rely on the men he had placed his trust in to help him rescue Sorcha and save his kingdom.

He simply never imagined the latter would come before the former.

CHAPTER TWENTY-THREE

Sorcha

Sorcha paced around the Unseelie castle for so long she felt sure she would erode the stone floor beneath her feet. The place seemed almost empty, devoid even of its usual ghostly whispers, stretching shadows and glimmers of silvery light. She knew why this was, of course.

Eirian had left to attack the Seelie Court.

But three days had passed since he had made the decision to preemptively strike his northern brethren. Sorcha was still struggling to come to terms with *why*, not least because the Unseelie king had not answered any of her questions – nor indeed spoken to her at all – since laying the revelation that she was pregnant at her feet.

With his child.

A sudden urge to be sick rolled over Sorcha. If she was being honest the baby-induced nausea and stabbing pains had entirely subsided over the last two days, which meant the only reason Sorcha felt sick at all was because of the situation in which she became pregnant.

In my bouts of memory loss he touched me, she thought, close to tears. Sorcha had either been on the verge of tears or full-on sobbing ever since she found out what had happened to her. *He perverted my mind and violated me. And now...*

She gulped down a fresh wave of tears, though the lump in her throat made it difficult for Sorcha to breathe. But she could not cry – not anymore. The baby growing inside her was *hers.* She had to cling to that even as she wished to violently reject the foreign life in her womb.

"My child, my child," she mumbled, over and over again. "My child, not his."

Sorcha knew Eirian would never let that be. The babe was his heir and, going by the way he'd reacted to the news of Sorcha's pregnancy, the Unseelie king had never reasonably expected such a thing to happen. *Lachlan did say it was difficult for faeries to conceive,* she thought. *But I did not realise it was as hard as this. And if it is so hard...*

Why was it so easy with me?

Before she knew it Sorcha found herself wandering through the hot springs, folding her legs beneath her to sit by the edge of the steaming water. She breathed in deeply, feeling her heart rate finally begin to slow to a far less tumultuous rate. But the sight of the water made her deeply unhappy, for it made her think of Murdoch.

"My second child I swore to you," she whispered, gazing at her hazy reflection in the hot springs. "Just as I failed Lachlan I have failed you."

Somewhere deep inside Sorcha knew that neither Murdoch nor Lachlan would have deemed her a failure. Their love for her – her love for *them* – was far too strong for a string of broken promises to destroy. But with Eirian descending upon the Seelie Court even as Sorcha bit back another round of tears she could not help the thought that both the kelpie and the Seelie king would have been better off if they'd never met her.

They would tell me I am foolish to believe such a thing. But it was foolish of them to love me in the first place.

It was foolish of me to love them.

"But I love you anyway," Sorcha said, swirling a finger through the hot water. It made her realise how cold her own skin was, for it stung her like a thousand needles. But she put up with the pain, drawing patterns through the water akin to the way Murdoch's form stretched and receded whenever he willed it to within the loch. Sorcha wished for nothing more now than to be enveloped in his embrace, when she was cold and frightened and felt very, very small. The kelpie of Loch Lomond had always looked out for her. Always protected her.

Sorcha had tried to return the favour – sacrificing her life for his – and now he could no longer look out for her.

She had never felt so miserable.

"*From ev'ry joy and pleasure torn,*" she whispered, still swirling the water. The song had been in her head for months now. The one she had sung to Murdoch, the night she'd tried and failed to betray him. If she squinted she could almost see dark shapes forming around her fingertip, so she sang to them.

"*Life's weary vale I'll wander thro';*

And hopeless, comfortless, I'll mourn,

A faithless woman's broken vow!"

Sorcha stared at the water beneath her, unblinking, imagining through her bleariness that the dark shapes she thought she could see through the steam were Murdoch himself. But then she frowned.

She *could* see Murdoch. In his true form.

With a gasp Sorcha realised the steam all around her had begun to dissipate, and the water right in front of her had become mirror-clear despite her breaking its surface with her finger. She lowered her hand further into the water, fruitlessly trying to grasp at strands of Murdoch's midnight-coloured mane before a heavy object knocked him to the ground.

He let out a scream, though it was tinny and insubstantial through the water, then with some effort shoved whatever had hit him off his back. There were glints and flashes around him as he ran that were not silver, like the Unseelie, but orange and red and *burning.*

There is fire around him.

Sorcha did not know what she was seeing. She had never witnessed a prophecy before – she was not sure she even believed them. And if her vision was wishful thinking then why would Sorcha have imagined Murdoch running through a wall of flame?

"Murdoch," she said, very quietly, then louder she

repeated it. "Murdoch. Murdoch. Murdoch."

The kelpie paused in his tracks. "...Sorcha?"

She could not believe it. What Sorcha was seeing was not a prophecy, nor a fantasy created by her brain.

She was seeing the present.

CHAPTER TWENTY-FOUR

Murdoch

"Lachlan!" Murdoch coughed, shifting a fallen tree off his back with a sharp twist of his shoulder. "Julian! Where are you?"

All around him was smoke and steam and cloying, burning soot. It filled Murdoch's lungs, stealing his very breath as he pushed away the tree trunk and struggled to his feet. Julian had not been joking when he said his fires could get large; for the first time Murdoch entertained the notion that they were perhaps too large for even him to quell.

No, he thought, shaking out his mane as he fled through the burning forest, willing the loch and its tributaries to douse the fires behind him. *I cannot lose faith now. Our plan is working.*

Though Murdoch had not seen the Unseelie king even once, he had torn apart dozens of his ghouls and twisted, ugly soldiers over the past hour. He only extinguished the fire around him when he was sure the area was empty.

All he had to do was listen to his enemies' anguished screams as they burned to death. When they, too, were extinguished, so too was the fire.

But Murdoch was tiring. He would go on - *had* to go on - for as long as it took, but such a broad-ranged attack was draining beyond belief. The kelpie had never had to deal with such vicious fires before.

He hoped never to have to do it again.

"...doch. Murdoch. Murdoch. Murdoch."

He froze. Was he imagining things? For through the haze of the burning fire - the cracking of wood, the screaming of faeries, the rush of the flames - Murdoch almost thought he could hear...

"Sorcha?" he wondered aloud, thinking he must be going mad.

Out of the corner of his eye Murdoch noticed a flash of silver just a moment too late. A bug-eyed, grotesque monster of an Unseelie had taken advantage of his momentary distraction to aim their cavernous maw right at his throat. The kelpie steeled himself for the blow, but the attack never came.

A blur from the right came crashing into the creature, snarling and snapping at their twisted skin until the Unseelie grew silent. When Murdoch spied a pair of startlingly amber eyes he relaxed.

"A wolf in more than name," he said, taking a few careful steps towards the hulking, long-limbed wolf that stood before him. Wordlessly the two animals that were not animals gently touched their noses together, blood dripping from Adrian Wolfe's wicked teeth as he smiled at Murdoch.

There was a wound on the wolf's left flank, though Adrian did not seem to mind it. He stalked around Murdoch the way he had done the first time they met, clearly searching for injuries upon the kelpie, then stopped in front of him then it became apparent his search brought up naught.

"A tree fell on me," Murdoch said, "but such a trivial thing cannot harm me. How are you faring, Wolfe?"

But Adrian did not reply, tongue lolling from his mouth as he stared at the kelpie. It occurred to Murdoch that the man may well not be *able* to speak in his animal form. He was a mortal, after all.

With no warning but a flick of his bushy tail Adrian bolted back through the forest the way he came, following the scent of blood that was pervasive upon the air. Murdoch allowed himself to admit that he need a minute to gather himself together again so, after a final glance at the ugly remains of the Unseelie Adrian had felled, he headed for the nearest burn that ran into Loch Lomond.

The water was a welcome slash of icy coolness against the suffocating, dry heat of the smoke. Murdoch dipped his muzzle into it, gratefully gulping down mouthful after mouthful of the stuff before treading his hooves through the bed of the stream. But as he moved an odd detail in the water caught his eye.

"No, it can't be..." he murmured, darting his head around to check that he was defiitely alone before peering down into the burn. "There is no way that—"

"Murdoch! Oh Murdoch, can you hear me?" came a voice that was unmistakably, impossibly Sorcha's. But before his eyes was her watery image, hair wild and tangled around her pale, astounded face.

Murdoch slipped into his human form in an instant, not caring for the way the water of the burn nipped at his naked skin to remind him that human flesh burned just as badly through ice as it did flame. He reached a hand out to Sorcha's face. He felt nothing but water, of course, but when she closed her eyes and cried out happily he could almost imagine the sensation of her cheek beneath his fingertips.

"How are you...is this real?" he asked, not daring to believe that it was.

But Sorcha nodded. "I spoke your name to the hot springs in the depths of the Unseelie castle, and sang you a song, and there you were! I thought you were a figment of my imagination but you're not, are you?"

"Not unless we are both imagining each other," Murdoch said, feeling a giddy urge to laugh.

A smile grew across Sorcha's face, mirroring the one Murdoch found his own lips curling into. "Murdoch, I have missed you so! It has been a torment unlike any other to be without you – to fall asleep in an empty bed, and sit by the fire alone, and keep songs within me instead of singing them for you."

"We will save you," Murdoch insisted. He leaned his face closer to the stream, wishing he could reach through the water and steal Sorcha away when nobody was watching. "*I* will save you. Just wait and see."

Sorcha's face softened at his words, but then quickly grew hard and serious. "What is going on in the Seelie

Court? Eirian—"

"We are handling it," he insisted. "We are winning. Lachlan's fire wizard finally came through for us. We are burning the vile Unseelie to ash."

To his surprise Sorcha did not look happy at all. Rather, a fleeting moment of heartbreak crossed her face, looking for a moment as if she would cry. "The forest," she murmured. "All the creatures within it. They will die, too."

A pang of sympathy and pure, unadulterated love hit Murdoch. He let out a short laugh. "Of course you are worried for the forest. But I am minimising the harm that comes to it, I swear it. The forest will regrow – Lachlan and Ailith will see to it that it happens as quickly as possible. So do not worry, Sorcha. We will best Eirian and then we will—"

Murdoch paused. He could hear a scuttling upon the earth to his left, and a soft stalking on his right. He had spent too much time focused on his impossible communication with Sorcha, and if he did not cut it off now then he would be in serious trouble.

"I must go," he said, hating every word as he rose to his feet. "I have to fight. I love you, Sorcha. I love you, I love you."

Panic crossed her face even as the very lines of it began to ripple and fade away. "I have to tell you something!" she cried. "Eirian, he – I am—"

But the rest of her sentence was lost to the sound of snapping teeth as a cat-faced Unseelie launched itself at Murdoch. He bodily kicked it away, still in the form of a man, and in the second it took the creature to recover Murdoch became a kelpie once more and trampled the faerie to death.

When the source of the scuttling – a grotesque, many-legged, scarlet-horned imp – came upon Murdoch he made quick work of it, too. But then another Unseelie came through the trees, fully engulfed in flame, aiming an attack at him even as their flesh was burned asunder. Several more followed, and before Murdoch had a chance to process where each enemy was coming from he was overrun with opponents to destroy.

Mustering all the concentration he had, he began to fill the Unseelie soldiers' lungs with their own blood, using the same trick he had used at the winter solstice revel five years prior. They choked and gagged, but still their attack did not relent.

It was therefore to his relief when Adrian leapt from the trees, pinning down a faceless, burning faerie despite the wolf's proclaimed fear of fire. Julian Thorne was not far behind, his scarlet robes stained black with soot and smoke. He looked exhausted beyond belief, as if a gentle push to his chest would knock him to the ground. But still he joined the fray, blasting the Unseelie with balls of fire so hot they burned blue.

"Thank you," Murdoch mouthed, before returning his attention to the stream of monsters intent on destroying him.

So absorbed in the onslaught was he that the kelpie did not have the time to think, even once, about what Sorcha had been trying to tell him.

CHAPTER TWENTY-FIVE

Lachlan

All around Lachlan was smoke and fire and death. It permeated the air, leaving him blind and deaf in a torrent of danger. He had to find a way through it.

He had to reach the Unseelie king.

"Where are you, silver bastard?" Lachlan bellowed, taking one of his favourite mortal curses as his own. "Come and fight me! That is what you're here for, isn't it?"

He did not expect Eirian to reply, of course, but the screaming and goading fired up Lachlan's fury until it burned hotter than the forest around him. He wiped away a fine sheen of sweat from his brow before it could reach his eyes; when he pulled his hand away it was black with soot.

"If only Clara could see me now," he coughed, almost laughing. "This is most definitely a sorrier state than being a fox ever was."

Fuelled by anger and a desire to steal back Sorcha once and for all, Lachlan powered on through the forest. When an Unseelie attacked – a beautiful faerie, dressed in silver armour engraved with fine scroll work and shards of diamond – Lachlan wasted no time in felling him with the blackened iron sword which had, once upon a time, been used by Murdoch-as-Lachlan to murder King Eirian's brother and nephew.

Lachlan felt it only fitting to use the same weapon to extinguish the final member of the Unseelie king's family.

When another equally beautiful faerie attacked him – a woman, this time – Lachlan kicked her in the stomach and commanded her to become one with the earth. His voice dripped power; the Unseelie, horrified, realised too late that she did not possess the ability to defy him. With a wretched scream she collapsed to her belly and dug and dug and dug at the ground, filling her mouth with soil until her scream was quelled. Lachlan watched with sickening satisfaction as the light from the creature's eyes disappeared.

"That was impressively cruel, fox king," an echoing, magically enhanced voice said.

Eirian.

Lachlan's long ears struggled to pinpoint the origin of the voice. But he followed his instincts and, though it involved fighting through the thickest licks of flame that enveloped the forest, he blindly clawed his way through to a clearing in the trees.

When he reached it, the space was completely devoid of smoke and carnage.

The pine trees circling the clearing were lush with green needles so dark they were almost black, and there was a fine layer of frost upon the ground that had covered the entire forest but two hours ago. The air smelled of cold, and winter, and life put on pause, and was startlingly, completely silent.

Beneath the empty boughs of an oak tree that was waiting for spring stood the Unseelie king himself, dressed in armour even more impressive that the kind his soldiers had been wearing.

The faerie smiled at Lachlan, all sharp teeth and ill intent. "Why, it appears you have found me alone and unarmed. Whatever will I do?"

Lachlan did not need his fox nose to smell a trap. His hand tightened around the leather-bound hilt of his sword, testing its weight as he took careful step after careful step towards Eirian.

The Unseelie king's smile only grew wider. "It seems your Court mislikes the fire as much as my poor army does. Tell me, Lachlan, how much energy will it take to restore your home? Far too much to employ a counter-attack against me, I would presume. Too much to even think of stealing back your unfortunate mortal love."

Lachlan bristled at the comment, though it relieved him to know that Eirian seemed to have no idea he managed to meet with Sorcha earlier in the year. But then he realised what the Unseelie king's first comment meant.

This entire attack was meant to maim us, not destroy us.

It made sense, of course. Eirian's numbers had been few, as Ronan predicted, and next to no direct attacks had been made on the palace. Most of the fighting seemed to be taking place directly in the forest; Lachlan himself ran into scarcely a handful of foes.

"If you think to injure us then you underestimate us," Lachlan said, using a touch of magic to clean the soot and sweat from his skin and clothes. His grip on his sword tightened as a result, though Eirian merely laughed.

"You are not even wearing armour, my dear Lachlan," he chided, throwing his arms open wide as if inviting an attack. "Are you even *trying* to best me?"

Lachlan dashed forwards to slash at Eirian's right hand, so quickly that it was all the faerie could do to just barely avoid the attack. "Armour slows me down," Lachlan snarled. "I have no doubt that I am faster than you."

"But are you stronger?"

Before Lachlan could strike another blow Eirian blasted him back with a burst of silver-rimmed magic. His eyes twitched, smarting at the sensation of the Unseelie's magic on his skin, before shaking himself out and attacking his opponent once again.

He was met with another blast.

"Your physical assault implies that you know your magic cannot beat me yet," Eirian said, gleeful as he stood and watched Lachlan fruitlessly try to reach him again and again. "And here I was, thinking you might have actually been some kind of match for me, after what dear Sorcha said about you."

"Do not speak her name!" Lachlan roared, furious.

But it was true that he doubted the strength of his magic; that he could control Eirian's armoured soldiers was a good sign, but the Unseelie king was hundreds of years old.

Lachlan knew in his heart that he needed Murdoch.

"Your kelpie cannot help you," Eirian said, silver eyes catching Lachlan's almost imperceptible look around him. "You will find that most all of your friends are, quite deliberately, otherwise engaged."

Damn it! Lachlan thought, stalking around to Eirian's left as he uselessly tried to find a weakness in the faerie's defence. It was clear that the Unseelie king had known exactly what he was doing from the start.

"You are making a direct attempt on mine and Murdoch's life," Lachlan said, aiming for a different tactic.

Eirian raised an eyebrow. "And? What of it?"

"You have broken the tenets of Sorcha's promise. By law you must release her!"

The laugh that was emitted from Eirian's mouth was manic. He threw his head back, near incapable of breathing through his mirth. "You are funny, fox king," he gasped. "You do not seriously believe that I will give her back, do you?"

"I have every right to rain fire upon your castle if you do not!"

"I would love to see you try." Eirian's laughter abruptly stopped, and his face grew serious. He took a step towards Lachlan, then another and another, crunching through frost with deliberate, slow movements. "Give her up, Lachlan. My claim on her is endlessly stronger than yours. I must profess my sympathies for your lost child, however. I would never rest in my quest for revenge if I were in the same position."

Lachlan froze. He was not supposed to *know* that Sorcha had lost their child. It was not difficult to feign horror and desperate disbelief at what he was hearing, much to Eirian's obvious enjoyment. "D-do not talk to me about family, you silver snake," Lachlan growled. "You know nothing of it."

He did not like the way Eirian kept coming closer, not a hint of fear in the faerie's eyes. He knew that Lachlan was not a threat to him. Not on his own. Not without back-up.

It had been his plan all along.

But when Eirian stood close enough to Lachlan to deal a killing blow, he paused.

Lachlan bared his teeth. "If you do not kill me now, I will strike back and destroy you in your sleep."

"How amusing," Eirian replied, eyes glinting as if they were made of the frost that covered the clearing. "Sorcha told me that if you ever meant her harm her kelpie would drown you in yours. The beast must be rubbing off on you, for you to have the same ideas of vengeance."

"Do not talk as if you know her – as if you regard her life as more than a bargaining chip against those that would otherwise destroy you!"

Eirian chuckled. "That is where you're wrong, my dear Lachlan. You are still so green. So much to learn. I think that, for her sake as well as your suffering, I will keep you alive for now. It would be a mighty shame if you did not see the events of the future unfold before your very eyes. This has been fun, fox king."

And with that he was gone. Lachlan hardly had the chance to blink before the Unseelie king disappeared, replaced by little more than a raven's feather.

Which means the defences are down around the Court, if he could magic his way out, Lachlan thought, too numb to process anything else Eirian had said as he stumbled back to the palace. Most of the forest around him was no longer aflame, but the damage had been done.

Everything was dead. It would take years to recover.

Lachlan forced himself to head towards the throne room instead of his chambers, though he was desperate to sleep. But he had no time to sleep – not when his entire kingdom was at stake.

He drowned his sorrows in half a pitcher of wine before Ronan showed up to stand in front of the throne, closely followed by Julian, Adrian and Murdoch. The entire group was covered in burns, soot and blood, blood, blood.

Lachlan could not tell if it was their blood or their enemy's.

"An ambush," Murdoch heaved. Julian was leaning heavily against his shoulder, barely conscious. "We might have lost, had Ronan not shown up in time."

"Four-and-ninety Unseelie ghouls, not afraid to burn and die," the horned faerie said. His eyes were blank; Lachlan had never seen him look so hollow. "They did not stop. They were mad. They were—"

"Enchanted, to stop the lot of you from helping your poor king."

Lachlan stilled. He did not recognise the voice. Nobody did.

Except Murdoch.

The kelpie turned to face a caped, shadowy figure lurking in the doorway. "In what world would you dare show your face in the faerie realm?"

"An opportunity arose that benefits both myself and your sorry group," the figure replied, stalking across the gilded floor of the throne room and parting the group standing before Lachlan in order to bow before him. "You have more need of what I have to say than you could ever know, King Lachlan."

He frowned. "Who *are* you?"

When the creature drew down their hood Lachlan was faced with silver, bulbous eyes, broken teeth and hair like seaweed. There was something familiar about them that he could not quite place; a memory of a story, perhaps, or a picture in a book.

And then it clicked.

"Beira," he said. "You are Beira."

The witch grinned a crooked, hideous grin. "That was my name, before. I would like it to be my name again."

CHAPTER TWENTY-SIX

Murdoch

"Beira?" Murdoch asked, more a question than a statement. It was a name he had not heard in quite some time. A name that wrought fear in faerie kind, and the humans who were unfortunate enough to cross her path.

"My mother cast you out," Lachlan said, frown deepening as he leaned forwards on his throne to inspect the wretched creature standing before him. "And then your own kind did, too. *Eirian* banished you. Someone get Ailith - she knows the history of this witch better than I."

Beira cackled. "I do not need a reminder of what I have done. Trust me, my former proclivities are where they should be: in the past. I am a changed witch, and I can prove it."

"I do not believe you."

"I cannot lie."

"And yet you are lying," Lachlan insisted, a fury rising in his eyes that Murdoch suspected had little to do with Beira herself and everything to do with the loss the Seelie Court had clearly just sustained. For if the tumultuous attack Murdoch, Julian and Adrian had faced was indeed an ambush, then...

That meant Eirian intended to face Lachlan alone.

And Eirian is still alive, which means Lachlan was not strong enough to defeat him on his own. But Lachlan *is alive, which means –*

"Why did the Unseelie king not kill you, fox?" Murdoch asked, cutting through the tension in the room with his question. He had no reason to distrust Beira, after all; she had only ever helped him. He did not mind getting answers from Lachlan in front of her.

The golden faerie stared at Beira, then at Murdoch. "This witch is your *friend*, isn't she? The one who told you how to—"

"To save your lovely lass," Beira said. "That was me. See? I want to help you; truly I do."

"You have never helped the Seelie before."

It was Ailith who had spoken, breathless in her rush to reach the throne room. There was blood on her hands and sapphire dress, though it did not belong to her. She shook her head sadly at Ronan. "Frederick will be fine, as will Jonas. Saoirse, on the other hand..."

The blank look on the horned faerie's face somehow got worse. Murdoch knew the Seelie Court had not been forced into fighting since before Lachlan's birth;

though Ronan had been glad for the excuse to strengthen their defences Murdoch somehow doubted the faerie had all that much actual combat experience.

"My role in the realm was never to help anyone - not directly," Beira said, responding to Ailith's first comment. "I was crucial in the building of our world. Our mountains. Our rivers. Our forests. I could see what others could not—"

"And used that to destroy what you saw fit!" Ailith snapped. Murdoch had not often seen the faerie irritated. It was an odd look upon her fair face. "You consumed mortals who were promised to members of our kind, transformed changelings into trees when you had no right to them, made moves to—"

"As I said before you appeared, Seelie queen," the witch said, her ugly voice masking all other noises in the throne room, "I do not need to be reminded of what I did in the past. More than a hundred years have passed, and I have learned my lesson. I truly am here to help, as the kelpie can attest to. All I want is a chance to return to the form and power I once possessed - that which is rightfully mine."

Against Murdoch's shoulder Julian had fully lost consciousness, and was beginning to fall to the floor. Adrian caught the man before he hit his head, easing him down to rest between them. It was bizarre to have Julian simply lie there, in the middle of the throne room, but for now it would have to do. Nobody wanted to miss part of the conversation, after all; that much was clear.

For a moment nobody said anything, then all eyes went to Lachlan. In this room - in this Court, in this kingdom - his word was law. Even Adrian Wolfe, who seemed inclined to follow his own rules as and when he liked, maintained a respectful silence instead of making a sly comment, though he glanced at Murdoch as if insinuating he expected the kelpie to say something.

But Murdoch had asked his question. It was up to Lachlan to answer it.

Eventually the Seelie king sighed, and slumped against his throne. "Eirian has something he wishes me to be alive to witness. Something for which I will *suffer*, it seems. I should not be surprised; that is his way of doing things. But he also..." Lachlan ran a hand over his face, then stared sightlessly at the ceiling. "He gave me his sympathies for the loss of my child. His sympathies! I am trying to see the jibe behind his words but I cannot. He said that there is nothing he would not do to get his revenge, were he in the same position as I am. What was his point in saying such a thing to me?"

"Because he is expecting an heir," Beira said, so matter-of-factly it took Murdoch entirely by surprise.

"You cannot mean that," Lachlan scoffed. "Surely not. Is this in the future? Is it something you have seen?"

"It is something I have seen but it is also something that is current. The Unseelie king is indeed going to, finally, become a father."

"And who is the mother? Who is—"

"*No.*"

The word came out of Murdoch before he could stop it, for now that he was no longer facing an assault on all sides by vicious, murderous foes he remembered his conversation with Sorcha. She had tried to tell him something.

Something important.

Something to do with Eirian.

When Beira nodded Murdoch collapsed to his knees. But Lachlan was still a few seconds behind Murdoch's revelation, so the kelpie was witness to every moment it took the fox to understand what Beira was insinuating.

"No!" he shouted, so loudly Julian groaned from his position sprawled across the floor. Lachlan got to his feet, a terrible expression on his face as he closed the gap between himself and Beira. He towered over her hunched, decrepit figure, yet she did not seem at all perturbed by the menace presented before her.

"Clara is not carrying his child. That is not what you are saying. There is no—"

"But this is good, isn't it?" Adrian chimed in, entirely unwelcome on all fronts.

"How *dare* you say that!" Lachlan snarled, just before Murdoch could say the same thing.

The amber-eyed man shrugged. "Did your witch friend's solution to taking Sorcha Darrow back not involve her being pregnant? Or did I misremember that?"

Murdoch stared at the man, then at Lachlan. He was right. To hear that Eirian had laid hands on Sorcha was an unimaginable nightmare. Murdoch could not fathom the pain she must be in. But the fact that she was carrying a child was the miracle he and Lachlan had been waiting for.

"You wish your form and power restored, you say?" Lachlan said, very quietly.

Beira grinned. "This information is surely worth it, fox king. Or have I overestimated the lass' value?"

"You have not. But—"

"Lachlan," Ailith said, voice full of warning. Murdoch watched as the two of them exchanged a meaningful look.

"Trust me," Lachlan said, before turning back to Beira. "I will grant you what you wish, but on two conditions."

The witch nodded. "Name them."

"We must successfully take Sorcha Darrow back from Eirian and, once we do, you must help protect her from him. This naturally involves you helping the Seelie Court as and when we need you."

"I am happy to agree to such terms, so long as helping the Seelie Court never interferes with the safety and wellbeing of the kelpie and his loch." She cast her bulbous gaze to Murdoch. "We are friends, after all."

An unexpected surge of affection hit Murdoch. Clearly he had underestimated how much the witch had valued his company over the years. He would be sure not to make the same mistake again; it was a good feeling to have someone fighting in the same corner as him... even if it was an Unseelie.

"Then we have reached an agreement," Lachlan said. "Somebody please take Julian to a bed and heal his mental trauma. Everyone else...sleep well. You will need all the rest you can get." Though Lachlan's voice was solid and determined Murdoch could not mistake the distress he saw in his eyes. The faerie would not sleep tonight, he knew. He would only think of Sorcha, and the child growing inside her that was not his.

Or mine, Murdoch thought, growing despondent in a moment. *Though Beira said Sorcha would have my child, that will not come to pass. It is impossible. I fear it means Beira's plan to save her will not work.*

But the kelpie did not vocalise his fear. They *needed* Beira's plan to work, after all.

He could deal with her being wrong about his son if it meant they saved the woman he loved.

CHAPTER TWENTY-SEVEN

Sorcha

Sorcha didn't know what was making her stomach roil and twist more - her pregnancy or the sight of Eirian torturing a broken-winged Seelie messenger in front of her.

"Does he really think I will communicate with him right now?" Eirian crooned, before stabbing the Seelie's stomach with a scalding hot iron. The creature screamed; their eyes cried red, red, red.

Sorcha wished she could put them out of their misery.

"His fire wizard may have successfully kept my ghouls at bay, but the fox could not best *me*," the Unseelie king continued, as if nothing out of the ordinary was happening whilst he spoke to Sorcha. "He is not strong enough. And your horse was not there to help him, nor his mortal friends. Rest assured Lachlan will not get a second chance to face me."

Eirian twisted the iron in his hands, pushing it further into the messenger's stomach. With a final, guttural cry the Seelie collapsed to the floor. Whether they were dead or simply unconscious, Sorcha could not tell.

"Why are you making me watch this?" she asked the cruel, silver king as he dropped the iron poker, removed the leather glove he'd worn to hold it, and turned his back on his prey.

He stalked towards Sorcha, sliding a hand across her stomach when he reached her even as she tried to flinch away. "Our child must see what their kind are capable of," he said. "They must grow used to the screams and cries of their enemies, for in the blink of an eye they will be ruling alongside me."

"I will *never* let that happen," Sorcha growled, once more attempting to move away from Eirian. But he grabbed at her cheeks with a grip of steel, preventing her from leaving.

"I do not see how you can stop me," he said, soft and sinister. He let go of her face, but with the Unseelie king's mercurial eyes so close to hers Sorcha found she no longer had the power to walk away from him. "Like it or not, lass, you are the mother of my child," he continued. "My heir. That makes you important above all others, and I would never dream of parting you from the babe. But mark my words, Sorcha: if you dare attempt to flee, I will hunt you down. I will scour the realm, and every corner of the earth we walk upon, until you are mine again, and you will be imprisoned in a corner of my kingdom until the end of time."

Silence. Sorcha could do nothing but return Eirian's stare.

"But we will not let it come to that," he said an interminably long time later, sickeningly cheerful again in the blink of an eye. He placed a gentle kiss on Sorcha's lips - a mockery of an affectionate gesture. "You will be my queen, if you only let me crown you. You need not suffer forever."

Considering what being Eirian's queen entailed, Sorcha rather preferred the option of being locked up until darkness permanently shrouded the earth and snuffed out her life for good.

Save me, she thought, feeling entirely hopeless when Eirian finally gave her leave to return to her chambers. *Somebody save me.* It did not matter who. If Sorcha could save herself she would, but she had no options left to her.

Eirian had proven he was stronger than Lachlan, and the Seelic Court was in ruins. Sorcha had witnessed but a fraction of the damage the fire had caused through her communication with Murdoch; it would take many years to restore its power.

Sorcha had to entertain the idea that the kelpie may well not be strong enough to battle head-on with Eirian, either, though now that the Unseelie king had attacked him he was free to respond in kind. She dearly did not want to lose Murdoch to Eirian, regardless if that meant Sorcha had to spend the rest of her life imprisoned by the faerie.

When she reached her room Sorcha spied one of the numerous hair pins Eirian had gifted her, laying innocuous on an ash table by the bed. Lilacs and bluebells and fronds of ivy, immortalised in silver and painted enamel. The sharp end of the pin gleamed wicked and inviting in the firelight.

"No," she murmured, trembling fingers grasping at the beautiful ornament as she stared down at her stomach. "I always have a way out."

But then she dropped the hair pin, numb to the sound of it clattering against the floor. Sorcha could not do it – could not even fathom the notion of taking her life when she held another within her.

The babe might have been Eirian's, but it was also hers.

Her child. *Her* responsibility. *Her* joy.

Nobody would take that from her...not even the creature who had forced his warped version of love upon her and taken away every choice Sorcha ever had in the matter of becoming a mother.

CHAPTER TWENTY-EIGHT

Lachlan

"We will only have this one shot."

"Yes, and you will succeed."

"You really think so?"

"I could not say it if I thought it were false, could I?"

Ailith's hand slid over Lachlan's and squeezed his fingers. In the darkness, beneath the sheets, with but a glimmer of light accentuating his queen's startling eyes and ice-blonde hair, Lachlan was reminded of a time gone by. All he'd had was Ailith. All she'd had was him.

Things were endlessly more complicated now.

Lachlan did not think either of them would change the circumstances of their current relationship even if they could. Ailith had Tomas – a soft-spoken, curly-haired faerie who provided Ailith with a settled love Lachlan could have never given her. And Lachlan...

No matter where she was, or who else she loved, Lachlan had Sorcha Darrow. The girl with the mismatched eyes. The girl with the voice of a silvered bell, or water over stone, or the wind through the trees.

The girl who was once, and always would be, Clara.

"We will save her," Lachlan said, to assure himself as much as Ailith. He kissed her brow when she closed her eyes. "The horse and me both. We will bring her back."

Ailith smiled. "Then be gone, my king. Do not return without her."

Lachlan did not waste much time in getting dressed before leaving his chambers. He spent more time searching for the kelpie, who did not seem to be anywhere in the palace. He spared a moment to check in on Julian, who after spending five solid days asleep was finally conscious once more.

"What are you doing, lurking within your own abode?" the wizard asked when he spied Lachlan by the doorway through a slitted, curious eye.

"I did not wish to rouse you from your rest," Lachlan replied simply.

Julian snorted. "I have slept quite enough, thank you. Evie would kill me if I slept through your rescue attempt. She will demand a minute-by-minute recount the moment I return to her."

"There won't be much to tell her about the hours you will have to sit here, waiting to see if the kelpie and I return empty-handed."

"Then I guess I can while away my time asking Wolfe

to tell me everything I have missed," Julian said, wincing at the notion of talking to his not-quite-friend. Then he pointed behind Lachlan, smiling slightly. "You should not tarry much longer, Lachlan of the Seelies. Save Miss Darrow, so that I may finally meet her."

Lachlan nodded, turning from the room without saying goodbye. Upon the advice of a guard he left the palace and passed through the revel clearing. The space had, miraculously, been saved from the fire, though just a few feet out of the clearing everywhere was a mess of burned, broken trees and blackened ferns.

It will take a lot of magic to encourage quick regrowth, he thought, pausing a moment to lay his hands upon the scorched earth. He could feel a pulse within it – a sign that it was not quite dead. He smiled grimly. *It will take a lot, but we can do it. The Seelie Court is strong. The forest is strong.*

Lachlan would not let Eirian destroy everything he held dear.

Almost two hours passed before Lachlan reached the waterfall pool where Murdoch Buchanan had first revealed himself to be a kelpie. He was lying beside the water in his true form, seemingly deep in silent conversation with Adrian, who was a wolf.

"I thought he couldn't speak in that form?" Lachlan asked, announcing his presence.

The kelpie whinnied softly. "He can't, but we understand each other anyway."

"Are you ready?"

"If I wasn't it would not matter; we need the distraction of the solstice revel in order for this to work."

With a shake of his head Murdoch got to his feet,

intimidatingly tall and fearsome beneath the midnight moon on the darkest night of the year. Adrian stood, too, giving Lachlan a wolfish grin before loping off into the forest on silent paws.

"Has he told you how he can become a wolf?" Lachlan asked, when he was sure the man was well out of earshot.

"Something to do with the remnants of a curse he can now activate at will," Murdoch replied. "It does not harm him the way it did before, so he no longer has to worry about losing himself to the beast. What is wrong?"

Lachlan realised he was grimacing at the kelpie, and had taken a step away from the creature. "I do not like it when you talk in this form," he admitted. "It is... unnerving."

Murdoch grinned, though it was all impossibly sharp, gleaming teeth and entirely terrifying. "Good," he said. "I am supposed to be unnerving. Now get on my back before I think better of this plan and buck you off."

"You could lower yourself to the ground to make this easier..." Lachlan muttered as he struggled to reach the kelpie's mane. Murdoch merely flicked his ears in response and, when Lachlan finally had but a tentative grip on the kelpie, hurtled off to the shore of Loch Lomond.

"Are you trying to kill me?!" Lachlan gasped, just barely managing to keep hold of Murdoch's mane. With some difficultly he launched himself onto the kelpie's back, kicking his heels into the creature's haunches in deliberate protest.

"You would know if I was trying to kill you."

"Drown me in my sleep?"

Murdoch glanced back at Lachlan, who could see himself reflected clearly in the kelpie's huge, coal-black eye. "What makes you say that?"

"Apparently Clara told Eirian that you would kill me in such a way, if I ever meant her harm. Was she speaking the truth?"

"I do not deny it," Murdoch replied, somewhat amused. "Though I would also consider crushing you beneath my hooves or ripping your throat out with my teeth."

"Charming. How did Clara know of this?"

"Because I told her, of course."

Lachlan all but choked in disbelief. "Is that what the two of you discussed in the Darach house, in your never-ending conversations by the fireplace?"

The briefest of hesitations. "I may have promised Sorcha I would kill you if you hurt her by the fireplace once or twice."

"And she simply *let* you?"

Murdoch snorted. "Hardly. It is gratifying to hear she remembered what I said, though."

"For you, perhaps."

"Perhaps. Are you ready?"

Lachlan realised they had reached the shore of the loch the instant before Murdoch stopped before it. He gritted his teeth, for he did not relish the thought of storming through lochs and rivers and seas with the kelpie.

In order to reach the Unseelie Court unseen, he had to.

"I am always ready for Sorcha," he said, reverting to her real name. "You remember what you need to do when we get there?"

"Focus on finding her," Murdoch replied, taking a few steps into the loch as he did so. The night air was freezing upon Lachlan's face; he shuddered to think of how cold it would be beneath the surface of the loch. "Do you believe Beira spoke true, when she said Eirian would focus solely on your presence?"

Lachlan nodded. "As far as anyone knows he does not realise there is a way for us to permanently take Sorcha from him, otherwise he would most definitely have killed me when he could. Better I distract him than the other way around."

A pause. "And what if he kills you, fox? Then there will be nothing stopping him following me and Sorcha and taking her back whenever he pleases."

"Do not consider me that weak. And besides...I trust you. To keep her safe, at least."

Another pause. "Likewise. But let's not have it come to that."

Lachlan barked out a laugh. "Yes, I would rather not die tonight. Now come on; let us save Sorcha Darrow."

CHAPTER TWENTY-NINE

Sorcha

Something woke Sorcha abruptly from her unsettled sleep. A noise. A disturbance.

A crash.

"I thought the revel didn't take part in the east wing of the castle...?" she wondered blearily. Stumbling slightly Sorcha got out of bed and made her way to the west-facing window – the one that looked over at the tower containing Eirian's chambers. There was light coming from his room, which seemed strange given that the Unseelie king was supposed to be at the revel.

Sorcha had declined to go, of course, and though it was clear Eirian was not pleased by this there was nothing he could do to force Sorcha to go without risking hurting the baby growing inside her. It was an unexpected, welcome perk to being pregnant with the heir to the Unseelie throne; Sorcha could not be harmed or drugged or otherwise put in a physically compromising situation.

"What is he doing in his chambers instead of the revel, then?" she wondered, concerned and curious. The winter solstice was the most important date in the Unseelie calendar, and after their apparent loss at the hands of the Seelie it was more vital than ever that Eirian demonstrated his strength and reliability as a king to his subjects.

They did not know his true intentions behind his attack on the Seelie Court, after all. They did not know that their king had done exactly what he intended to do...even if that came at the cost of a hundred Unseelie lives.

With a sigh Sorcha wandered over to the mirror in her room, staring at it with every intention of being noticed by the watcher on the other side. "What is going on?" she demanded. And then, because he was more inclined to answer her if she framed it in such a way: "I will not have revellers anywhere near my baby."

It was to Sorcha's immense surprise when a long-fingered hand with nails filed to points – Eirian's hand – appeared through the glass and pulled Sorcha through its surface. She flinched for but a moment, expecting to hit it, but then the moment passed and she found herself in a room entirely unfamiliar to her.

"So you were not in your chambers, then," she said, somewhat dazed. She looked around the barely-lit room, though aside from the aged and cracked mirror she had been pulled through there was nothing inside it.

Eirian was holding a candle in his other hand; he

held it up to illuminate his face as he pulled Sorcha close. "It seems we have intruders, though they should not have made it this far without being noticed."

Sorcha hardly dared to acknowledge the spark of hope that lit up her heart.

"Are you sure they aren't simply revel-goers who have lost their way?"

The look on Eirian's face suggested he was in no mood for such questions. In the candlelight she could see that his pupils were dilated, suggesting he was not in the least bit sober. A dark stain upon his shirt could have been wine, though Sorcha reasoned it could just as easily have been blood.

"So you *were* at the revel," she mused, ignoring the way Eirian's grip on her wrist tightened. "The light in your chambers – a ruse, then? What could you possibly be expecting to happen after you so decidedly decimated the See-"

"The gravity of your situation escapes you, it seems," Eirian cut in, turning from Sorcha to pull her along a corridor she had not been able to make out in the darkness. "If anyone has come to try and *save* you, mark my words, Sorcha: I will kill them. I will kill all who helped them."

Sorcha gulped despite herself. She had no doubt Eirian would do such a thing, and for the most part she sincerely wished the disturbance in the castle had been exactly what she suggested it might be: a lost reveller.

Yet somehow she could not find it within herself to feel truly fearful. The idea that Lachlan and Murdoch had so swiftly gotten back on their feet to launch an assault against Eirian was gratifying.

Encouraging.

"You will remain here for now," the Unseelie king said, letting go of Sorcha to light several torches set into sconces. With a glance at a grey-stoned fireplace the hearth burst into silver flames, taking the edge from the chill of the room in an instant. Below her feet the floor was covered by a threadbare rug, though the bed in the corner looked far newer and well-maintained.

"I am underground, aren't I?" Sorcha asked, certain.

"What does it matter where you are? You will not be able to leave."

"Then perhaps you underestimate me."

Eirian dropped the candle in his hand; its flame stuttered out of existence at his feet. Sliding a hand to the small of Sorcha's back, he pushed her against him until she had to crane her neck upwards to see his face. Without the candle's flame the faerie's pupils dilated even further, leaving but a sliver of silver around them.

Like an eclipse, Sorcha thought. *But the moon never hides the sun for long.*

"If you think I would so easily give you a chance to escape then *you* underestimate *me,* my foolish queen," the Unseelie king murmured. He bent his head, first placing a kiss upon Sorcha's brow, then the tip of her nose and, lastly, her lips. She went rigid in his grip, trying desperately not to taste anything on his tongue when Eirian forced her mouth open to accept it, lest he had been drinking faerie wine. But the kiss was insistent and brutal; Sorcha could do nothing to reject it no matter how hard she struggled.

When Eirian finally broke away a smirk pulled at the corners of his mouth. "I do not need faerie wine to keep you in here," he said, making for the corridor that led back to the crumbling mirror he had pulled Sorcha through mere minutes ago. "For you are without magic, and without magic you have no chance of breaking through a wall of stone."

Sorcha frowned at him. "A wall?"

His smirk became a grin. "Like this," he said, and clicked his fingers.

The opening to the corridor vanished and Eirian with it, though Sorcha could hear him cackling from behind the blockage. "I will enjoy our time together, once I have dealt with this *disturbance,*" he called through the stone. "You had best get some sleep whilst you still can."

When the sound of his footsteps receded into silence Sorcha threw herself against the wall with a roar of frustration. "I will not wait here for you to violate me as you see fit!" she screamed, banging her fists against the cold stone in front of her before collapsing to her knees in front of the silver fireplace. She stared into the flames, imagining Eirian within them, burning.

A rescue, she thought, after her rage had finally subsided. *I must have faith. I will wait for a rescue.*

There was nothing else she would willingly wait for.

CHAPTER THIRTY

Murdoch

"Sorcha, Sorcha, Sorcha," Murdoch uttered under his breath, over and over again as he searched wildly around for her. The Unseelie castle was cold and empty, since most all of its usual inhabitants were at the revel. The deluge of noise coming from the celebration had covered Murdoch's tracks as he carried Lachlan to the exact spot the faerie guided him to – a grille in the castle wall, where steaming water escaped into the cold, unforgiving forest behind them.

Lachlan had hoped Murdoch would be able to melt into the water, and him with it. But the stream of water had been far too small for him to properly utilise so, without thinking of the consequences, Murdoch had merely bowled straight into a fault in the wall once, twice, three times, until the stones gave way and he galloped through the resultant opening into the middle of a steam-filled underground forest.

The noise the kelpie made in entering the castle this

way had been tumultuous, but neither he nor Lachlan had the time to be angry with his approach. Without a word Lachlan had slid off Murdoch's back and vanished into the darkness in search of Eirian.

The kelpie changed into his human form, the better to navigate tunnels and stairwells. But after fifteen minutes of searching he found he could not make heads nor tails of the place, and had no hints as to where Sorcha might be.

I need her scent, he thought, shaking himself back into a kelpie once more. It made traversing through the castle far more arduous, and eventually Murdoch grew so frustrated he was tempted to simply bowl through every wall he saw until he found the room where Sorcha was hidden.

But he couldn't do that; a series of crashes and loud, furious gallops across hard stone floors would be far more of a distraction than Lachlan could ever be. Murdoch would be found and, with it, any chance he had of finding Sorcha.

"Where are you, Sorcha?" he whispered, creeping along a ground floor passageway after investigating a tower in the east wing. It had been full of Sorcha's scent, yet she was not in it. There was no trail from the tower, either, which meant Sorcha had been removed from the tower by other means.

Magical means.

She has to be here, Murdoch thought, growing ever more desperate as he rather inelegantly made his way down to the first basement level of the castle. The smell of the food stores overwhelmed his nose, so Murdoch retreated from them to travel further downwards. But the passageways were getting narrower and narrower; soon he would have to turn back into a man, and he would lose his acute sense of smell.

"A clue," he mumbled, nosing at the stones beneath him as he traversed a dark and dingy corridor. It ended at a gnarled door, which stood ajar, so with a butt of his head Murdoch pushed it open. Inside was a room that was just as sparse and dark as the corridor, but upon the wall...

There was a mirror.

And Murdoch could smell Sorcha.

The doorway was far too small for a kelpie to walk through, so Murdoch shifted back to a man as his pulse raced faster and faster. "Sorcha!" he cried, not caring when his voice reverberated back at him a thousand times louder than his initial shout. He was so close; he would not let Sorcha slip away by staying silent. "Sorcha, where are you?"

But the only reply he got was his own voice, then silence, so Murdoch stalked around the room searching for any sign of Sorcha's presence. When he realised a further corridor led off from the room he wasted no time in sprinting down it, knowing in his heart that Sorcha must surely be at the end of it.

It was a dead end.

"Damn it all to hell!" Murdoch yelled, slamming his hands against the wall. "Don't keep her from me, you snake! Give her back!"

"...Murdoch?"

He froze, listening intently. Murdoch had been sure he'd heard his name, just as he'd heard it back in the forest when everything was on fire.

"Sorcha?" he called, staring at the wall in front of him as if he could somehow see through stone.

"It's me!" she cried, filling Murdoch with relief. "You found me!"

"Where are you?" he asked, relief quickly replaced by urgency when he remembered he likely had very little time left before Eirian realised Lachlan had been naught but a distraction. "Behind the wall?"

A pause, then: "Yes! Yes, behind the wall. I actually nodded in answer first. How silly is that? I—"

"Oh, I love you," Murdoch said, a wide smile on his face for nobody to see but the wall. "I love you more than anything. Did Eirian magic you into there, Sorcha?"

"There was a door, at first. He walked me through, then removed the door when he left – or turned it into a wall. Does that make a difference?"

"All the difference in the world," Murdoch said, tapping upon the stone where a door might be. And, sure enough, the sound his knuckles made was not what he would have expected from a solid wall made of two feet of stone. "A wall this thick with no faults in the stone is difficult even for me to break," he murmured, continuing to tap across the wall to determine the dimensions of the door. "But one which is no true wall at all...stand back, Sorcha."

With a savage grin Murdoch backed away from the door, steeling himself for the tight fit of the corridor before transforming once more into a kelpie. He pawed at the ground, shifting his weight from one leg to the other, then hurtled down the corridor with all the speed he could muster.

When he hit the wall a resounding crack filled the

air, but it did not come down. Murdoch pushed against it again, then retreated down the corridor to charge a second time. The cracking grew louder, and the air filled with dust. One final shove and the wall crumbled, sending stones of all sizes skittering across the wall.

Murdoch could not see anything through the debris at first. He returned to his human form, coughing as dust filled his lungs. But then the air cleared, and a figure became visible in front of him.

"*Fair and lovely as thou art,*" Murdoch recited before he could stop himself, the words belonging to a song Sorcha used to sing to him. He kicked away the remaining stone that stood between him and the woman he had spent every day and night over the last nine months longing for.

"*Thou hast stown my very heart;*

I can die – but canna part,

My bonnie dearie."

Silence. The air completely cleared, and she came fully into view.

"You grew out your hair," Sorcha said, tears in her eyes as she stumbled into Murdoch's arms.

He could not believe she was here – that *he* was here, with her. Murdoch could not stop his hands from trembling, no matter how tightly he grabbed onto Sorcha. "You will have to cut it for me," he said, laughing. "But first – but first—"

Murdoch broke away from Sorcha just enough to tilt her chin upwards, marvelling at her green-and-blue eyes staring right back up at him, and kissed her. He kissed her like it was the first time he had ever kissed her, and the last time, and all the times in-between. If he could have his way Murdoch would have remained in that moment, kissing Sorcha Darrow until the end of forever.

A certain someone would never forgive him if he did.

He pulled away from the kiss and gently took Sorcha's hand in his, pulling her down the corridor as he did so. He flashed a grin at her she eagerly returned.

"First we have a fox to save."

CHAPTER THIRTY-ONE

Lachlan

"Do not dare take her from me, Lachlan."

"I wondered when you'd find me," Lachlan said, turning to face King Eirian as the silver faerie approached him. He pointed upwards. "I was going to look for you in your chambers, but of course you would not be there. The light in the window was a ruse."

"Which you were clearly too clever to fall for," Eirian replied, eyes glittering dangerously as he stalked around Lachlan even as Lachlan did the same to him. He gestured around them. "The courtyard seems as interesting a place as any to destroy you. Tell me: what did you expect to achieve by coming here?"

Lachlan chuckled. "Why, to prove that I am not too weak to best you, of course. And to tell you that I know."

The Unseelie king froze. "Know what, exactly?"

"Everything. I knew Sorcha lost our baby months and

months ago."

"You are—"

"Lying?" Lachlan cut in, continuing to prowl across the courtyard. He had to clear a path for Murdoch; he did not want to risk the kelpie bowling into Eirian on the off-chance the faerie was strong enough to cling onto him. "I am lying, you think? I do not have time to twist my words into half-truths and jibes like you do. No, I am being honest. I crept into your Court – into your castle – and spoke to Sorcha. She told me about the babe. About the fact you turned her *immortal*."

His final word was a snarl.

Eirian composed himself within the space of a blink. An easy smile spread across his face, and he flicked his hair over one shoulder. "It does not matter that you already knew. It does not matter at all. Your child is gone, Lachlan, and your mortal love, too."

"That she is not mortal may be true, but she is not gone," Lachlan replied, daring to take a step towards Eirian. With his keen eyes he could see the silver king was not in his complete and lucid mind. His pupils were far too dilated; his movements but a fraction too slow.

We were right to use the solstice as cover, he thought, viciously happy. *If his actions are slower then I can only hope his mind is slower, too.*

"You cannot have her," Eirian insisted, as if that was that and the matter was closed. "I have taken a liking to her. So leave, before I kill you for a girl you will surely forget in a hundred years or so."

"I know she's carrying *your* child, Eirian."

A flinch.

"You cannot know that."

Lachlan could only cackle the way Eirian always did. "A woman becoming pregnant at the hands of both faerie kings? You thought I could not know? Did you not consider that there must surely be one witch or sightseer or another who saw this happening?"

That Eirian did not immediately reply meant that he most certainly had. But that Lachlan had been the one to hear the prophecy, not him, was a blow against the Unseelie king's pride.

"And who, if you would care to divulge, was this visionary behind this auspicious event?" he asked, almost through gritted teeth.

Good, Lachlan thought. *Get angrier. Get sloppier. Get so involved in your rage you do not notice the kelpie thundering out of your castle until it is too late.*

"I think you may have heard of her, once upon a time," Lachlan said, thoroughly enjoying himself despite the gravity of the situation. "She was truly formidable. Terrifying. And she will be, again, because of me. It is most certainly a boon, to have Beira the Bloodthirsty in the service of the Seelie Court."

Eirian's eyes grew wide. "You are *lying.*"

"You seem fond of saying that, when it seems as if others know things that you do not. Are you really so arrogant as to believe not a single soul out there can outsmart you?"

"You have not *outsmarted* me, damn fox," Eirian said. He looked around the empty courtyard. "You came here alone, with the blind courage that you could somehow defeat me. But you can't, Lachlan. You are not strong enough."

"You are right," Lachlan replied, feigning sorrow. A rumbling beneath his feet told him it was time to leave. He took another step towards Eirian, then another and another, with fury in his eyes and a growl upon his lips. "I am not strong enough to defeat...yet. But I am not alone."

Finally, too late, Eirian took notice of the stones below him vibrating as if they were abuzz with energy. "What—" he began, but then the kelpie came crashing down the stairs, screaming and roaring as he seemed to all but fly across the courtyard.

Lachlan used Eirian's momentary distraction to push him away with a surge of magic, sending him tumbling backwards and well out of reach of Murdoch.

A hand extended down from the kelpie's back.

"Lachlan!" Sorcha cried. With the moonlight in her wild, copper hair, and the wind billowing the gossamer material of her dress, and the luminous look upon her face as she reached for him, Lachlan thought she looked altogether unreal. But she *was* real.

Lachlan took her hand.

"I'm sorry it took so long," he said, crushing Sorcha against his chest and clinging to the kelpie's mane in the process.

She let out a barely discernible sob. "You were just in time."

"*Bring her back!*" Eirian screeched, razor-sharp teeth bared and silver eyes flashing as his gargantuan raven-feathered wings unfurled into existence. "*Bring her—*"

But Murdoch ran faster than the Unseelie king could possibly contend with, and the end of Eirian's demand was lost to the wind.

Lachlan indulged the urge to pat the kelpie's neck as if he were a horse and not a monster. "Take us home, horse."

Murdoch snorted. "Do that again and I—"

"Shall drown me in my sleep," Lachlan said.

"Shall drown him in his sleep," Sorcha replied, at the same time.

And then, because no other words could describe what they had just gone through – what they had been going through for years, ever since Lachlan was first turned into a fox at the hands of his Unseelie stepfamily – Murdoch said, "Home it is."

CHAPTER THIRTY-TWO

Sorcha

Sorcha was barely given time to exhale before she was thrust into the overwhelming brightness of the Seelie Court. Lachlan and Murdoch blithely led her to one of the many drawing rooms, where several people already resided.

"Miss Sorcha!" Ailith cried, bodily throwing herself at her before Sorcha had an opportunity to respond. But she returned the embrace, feeling her throat begin to clog with tears when the faerie stroked her hair and openly wept.

"I am – I am here, Ailith," Sorcha said, choking on a laugh as she pulled away from her and saw her lovely face dripping with tears. "I made it back safe and sound. Well, sound, but are we safe?"

She turned her gaze to Lachlan, then Murdoch. "What is to stop Eirian from coming after me?"

Lachlan grinned. "We copied the circumstances upon which he stole you away. He has no right to claim you, now."

Sorcha considered this. It seemed ridiculous, to have been saved in such a way, but many faerie laws and customs seemed ridiculous to a mortal.

Not a mortal.

Her sudden ashen appearance was noticed in an instant by Murdoch. He reached for her, and pushed towards the fire. One of the two men who were sitting in armchairs by the hearth – both of them strangers – politely stood up and offered his chair to her. As he moved Sorcha caught a flash of amber, and she realised he was not a stranger at all.

"You," she said, losing all coherent speech for a moment. She forced her brain to work once more. "London. The coffee house. You told me to be careful, but not of Murdoch. Just who exactly are you?"

Lachlan, Murdoch and the remaining stranger stared at the amber-eyed man.

"You never told us you *met* her!" the stranger complained. "Not once, the entire time we were travelling to the faerie realm, did you mention this. Did you not think it prudent to tell me you had once run into Sorcha Darrow?"

The man shrugged. "What of it? It does not matter now. She was not careful, and she paid the price, but she is safe now."

"I would hold your tongue if you wish to keep it," Lachlan hissed. "Do not talk of—"

"Will you all calm down?" Sorcha demanded, exasperated but happy in equal measure. This kind of argument felt familiar. It was something she could deal with. "The man is right; I *wasn't* careful. I should have heeded your advice when you gave it to me, Mister...?"

"Wolfe," the man replied, bowing deeply. "Adrian Wolfe."

She smiled at the remaining stranger, who was still glaring at Adrian. "Which makes you Julian, the wizard. Please accept my deepest gratitude for saving Lachlan's life, seven years ago."

When Julian stopped glaring and granted Sorcha a smile she was taken aback by how handsome it made him. "It is a pleasure to meet you, Miss Darrow, though I wish the circumstances were better. How are you feeling?"

It was a strange question to be asked, though it was the most normal question in the world. "I - do not know," Sorcha replied. "Nine months ago I was mortal, and I was..." She gulped, flashing a look at Lachlan before staring into the fire to keep back her tears. Now that she was sitting down, and warm, and safe, Sorcha was beginning to find the circumstances of her life altgother far too overwhelming.

Behind her Ailith began stroking her hair once more, crooning softly as she often did when the two of them spent time together. It set Sorcha at ease, which she gratefully assumed was the point. She set a hand across her stomach. "Now I am pregnant once more, but it is not the babe I chose to have."

"We will get rid of it," Lachlan said, rushing to her side with eager eyes. "We can magic the babe away, Clara. You will feel nothing. No pain. We can—"

"*No!*" she cried, beyond horrified. "This is my baby. *My* baby. You will not take them away from me!"

"But Sorcha," Murdoch said, kneeling down in front of her, "you cannot have the baby. Eirian will—"

"You said I was safe!"

"Not if you have the baby! You cannot—"

"Do not tell me what I can and cannot do, after all that has happened to me!"

Sorcha began to hyperventilate; even Ailith's fingertips on her head could do nothing to calm her down. "I will not—" she gasped, "I cannot – to lose my mortal life and my baby – I will not let that stand!"

The look in both Lachlan and Murdoch's eyes was tragic. But they could not understand; they were not the ones carrying the life within her. It had been the only thing stopping her from ending her *own* life to escape Eirian's torment. She would give the child all the love in the world, to replace the entirely loveless way in which they were conceived.

"You would dare tell a woman to give up her child?"

Sorcha turned her head to face the door. A faerie she did not recognise stood there, impossibly beautiful and statuesque. Her hair was the colour of moonlight, and flowed down to her feet like a river. Her face seemed carved from marble of a similar colour to her hair, and her hands were elegant and long-fingered. Startling blue eyes shot through with silver gazed around the room in fury.

Lachlan frowned. "Who are—"

"You ask me to protect this girl from the Unseelie king," the faerie interrupted. "Do you doubt my powers to keep him at bay? She is carrying a babe who will one day *rule*. Sorcha Darrow will have her child and they will both be safe. You have my absolute word on the matter."

Out of the corner of her eye Sorcha saw a flash of recognition cross Murdoch's face. "Beira?"

The faerie nodded. "Returned to my true and rightful state, as promised by the Seelie king."

"You said...rule?" Sorcha asked the faerie.

"My visions do not lie. Your child will rule a faerie throne."

Sorcha still had no idea who the faerie was – her name meant nothing to her, and the accuracy of her visions even less so – but she was pleased to have such a commanding presence on her side. "If you would mean to protect me and my baby then I gladly accept your offer, Beira."

"As is only right," Beira said, satisfied. "The babe will need all the help they can get, with the fox and the kelpie around."

Both Lachlan and Murdoch looked as if they wanted nothing more than to complain, but found that they couldn't.

Murdoch sighed. "You are right, and I am sorry. Sorcha, I did not mean—"

"I know," Sorcha said, She turned her gaze to Lachlan. "Both of you. I know you only want to protect me. But this baby is not a threat to me; their father is. And I will *never* let Eirian near them, not for as long as I shall li–"

"Of course!" Adrian burst out, much to the surprise

of everyone currently discussing Sorcha's baby. All attention diverted to the magician.

He grinned a wolfish grin at Sorcha. "...I think I've worked it out."

"What do you mean, you *think you've worked it out*?" Lachlan asked, narrowing his eyes at Adrian. "Worked what out?"

"Your mortality issue."

"Which part of the conversation was about that?" Murdoch asked, deeply confused.

But to his right Julian cocked his head, a wave of understanding crossing his face. He turned to Adrian. "Like with the Greek girl and the king?"

Adrian nodded. "A counter-curse. A balance."

"What do you mean?" Sorcha asked, not daring to trust the excited gleam in the man's amber eyes. "What would you do to me?"

"Mortality to immortality, and immortality to mortality, can only happen once, am I correct?" the man asked Lachlan, who nodded. "Could you take someone else's opportunity to switch between the two?"

"The legend goes that when a mortal is made immortal, they steal the life from a faerie who was not using it, but I believed it to be nonsense," Lachlan said, "until Eirian cast the magic on Sorcha and she lost her half-faerie child. But that could simply be awful coincidence."

But Adrian shook his head. "Blood magic is never coincidence. Your legend may only hold true for women who carry another life within them."

Sorcha rushed to her feet immediately, heart racing

in fury. "I will not give up my—"

"You will not lose your baby," Adrian said, very patient. "But your baby will lose their ability to become mortal."

Sorcha faltered. "They – you can do that?"

"If you wish it to be so, I can do it."

All around her were murmurs of excitement. Murdoch in particular looked ecstatic by the prospect.

"I knew there was a reason I brought you with me, Wolfe," Julian muttered, which caused Adrian to roll his eyes.

"I can't," Sorcha said, causing gasps of disbelief all round.

"Sorcha," Murdoch said, taking her hands in his and squeezing them slightly too hard. "You cannot mean that. You—"

"I will not take my own child's right to choose away from them," she insisted, knowing it was the right move. "To do so would make me no better than *him*."

Adrian considered this. "Once the babe is born I cannot work the counter-curse. If we wait for the child to make the decision of their own accord it will be too late."

"But does the counter-curse have a time limit?" Julian asked. "Is it immediate, or can you—"

"Ah, I knew there was a reason I brought *you* with me," Adrian chuckled. "Miss Darrow, how about this: when you child comes of age – whenever that may be. When they are ready to rule, when they are ready to choose. When they are ready to forsake their chance for mortality. Then, and only then, will that chance be given to you."

"I..." Sorcha mulled the man's words. They were imbibed with magic, washing over her with their power and their promise. "Yes," she said. "Yes, I can agree to that."

"Oh, thank the forest," Lachlan breathed out, looking almost ready to collapse in relief. He ran a hand through his hair. "But they will *rule*? You are sure, Beira?"

The faerie gave him a look that suggested his question was an affront to her powers, which Sorcha imagined it was. "I am never wrong, as I have said at least once or twice before."

"I do not care if my child wears a crown or not," Sorcha said. "But what I do care about – what I want more than anything – is to get to my bed. *My* bed, in *my* house."

Without a word of warning Murdoch swept her up into his arms. "Then bed it is. Ailith, I don't suppose you could spare some magic to—"

"No need to ask," she said, smiling. "Simply take a step outside this room and you will be back in the Darrow house."

Sorcha grinned at Murdoch, then glanced at Lachlan. "If you go near my dreams tonight—"

"Murdoch will murder me."

"No, *I* will. I need to sleep for at least three days."

The faerie chuckled softly, for he understood what Sorcha was saying. *Not tonight, but sometime soon.*

Tonight was for Sorcha, and Sorcha alone.

She could deal with the beginning of the rest of her

life in the morning.

CHAPTER THIRTY-THREE

Murdoch

Murdoch could only watch as Sorcha rubbed a hand against her growing belly and sang softly. She was singing nonsense – made-up words and riddles with no answers – but her voice was so lovely that Murdoch's heart ached to hear it. There was a tenderness to it that he'd rarely heard before, in fleeting moments where she'd sing to Galileo when she thought nobody was listening. He wondered if the baby would inherit her voice.

He would be a dangerous faerie indeed, to inherit such a skill.

He had not once told Sorcha that he knew the baby would be a boy. That would involve telling her about the vision Beira had recited to him - that Sorcha would grant him a son within eighteen months and a day - and Murdoch did not want to put such pressures on the woman he loved. If Sorcha wished for Murdoch to help her raise her baby as his own child then it had to be *her* choice, not because of something a faerie witch had proclaimed.

To think Beira meant I would have an Unseelie son, of all things, Murdoch thought, edging closer to the fire to warm the ends of his fingers. It was a bitterly cold February evening; Murdoch and Sorcha were curled up in their favourite armchairs by the drawing room hearth.

Murdoch caught Sorcha watching him warm his hands with a slight smile on her face. She indicated towards one of several blankets covering her lap. "Take one of these if you are cold, Murdoch," she said. "I do not need them all." Going by the rosiness of her cheeks she was telling the truth.

But Murdoch shook his head. "Those are for the babe," he insisted. "We cannot risk h–them catching a chill." He just barely stopped himself from saying *him*; Murdoch inwardly cursed.

Be careful. Do not make Sorcha's pregnancy more stressful that it needs to be.

Murdoch suppressed a humourless snort of laughter. It was hard to imagine anything more stressful that being impregnated by the Unseelie king by way of faerie-fruit-induced hallucinations. It didn't help that Sorcha couldn't involve her mother with the baby's birth, either – not until the boy was born and Lachlan could work a glamour upon him to look truly human.

"What is on your mind?" Sorcha asked, catching the dark, troubled look that crossed Murdoch's face with practised ease.

He moved over from the fire to perch on the arm of

Sorcha's chair, squeezing her shoulder before gently kissing her forehead. "It is nothing," he said. "Just the usual worries."

"You are lying."

"I am not."

"You are!" Sorcha pressed, looking up at Murdoch with a frown on her face and a pout on her lips. It was so endearing that Murdoch found himself leaning down to kiss her properly before he could stop himself. Sorcha eagerly welcomed the kiss, wrapping her arms around Murdoch's shoulders to pull him insistently closer. Her mouth tasted of sugar and lemons – a remnant of the tart, sherbet-filled sweets Mrs Ferguson had sent up from London after Sorcha had requested them a fortnight ago.

When their lips finally parted Sorcha leaned against Murdoch's chest, sighing heavily. "Please tell me what it is that is troubling you so. You have had the same conflicted expression on your face for weeks now."

Murdoch hesitated for a moment. "I sincerely do not wish to push such matters on you when you—"

"*Murdoch.*"

It was his turn to sigh. "Fine," he said. "I give in." With gentle hands Murdoch pushed Sorcha away from his chest so he could look at her properly. Her green-and-blue eyes were bright and intent on his; Murdoch loved those eyes more than he could ever say. His grip tightened on her shoulders. "I – we have not discussed this yet, because I did not think it would be fair to do so, but—"

"You have never hesitated to say *anything* to me before," Sorcha cut in. "After knowing each other for so long just what is stopping you from saying what you think?"

Murdoch's gaze fell to her stomach. "The baby."

"What about the baby?"

"I..." Murdoch took a gulp of air and closed his eyes. His heart was hammering in his chest, making him feel altogether sick with nerves. "It is your baby and therefore your choice," he said, opening his eyes once more to find that Sorcha had cocked her head to one side and was biting her lower lip in curious confusion. "After everything you have been through – after every choice that has been torn from you – you have every right to tell me you do not want this."

Murdoch took another deep breath. "Sorcha Darrow, will you allow me to love and raise this child as my own? I know this was not the way we planned to have a baby together – that we may not get to have the family we wanted for a long, long time – but all I want is to raise this child with you. As *our* child."

An achingly long moment of silence stretched on for what felt like an age. Murdoch could read nothing from Sorcha's face, which only caused his heart to hurt even more. But then her eyes grew altogether too shiny, and she began to cry, and she ran a hand through Murdoch's hair to pull his lips back to hers once more.

"Of course, you idiot," she said, voice full of tears as she kissed him again and again and again. "I was beginning to think you would *never* ask me. Was so worried you wouldn't. I didn't want to push any responsibility onto you."

Murdoch wrapped his arms around her in delight. "We are both as bad as each other," he laughed. "We could have felt a whole lot better about this situation had we merely talked about it long before now."

"I did not know if you could love an Unseelie child," Sorcha admitted, the words muffled against Murdoch's lips. "Considering the circumstances in which I found myself pregnant—"

"Sorcha, it is *because* of those circumstances that I will love the babe more than anything," he interrupted, grazing his teeth along Sorcha's jawline as he did so. When Murdoch reached her earlobe he gently bit it. "How could I not love a child borne from the woman who means the world to me?"

The two of them said nothing for a while, content to plant lazy kisses on each other and embrace within the confines of Sorcha's armchair, but then the booming crack of the front door opening drove Murdoch immediately to his feet.

Sorcha looked at him with wide eyes before grabbing his hand. "Who on earth could it be at this – Lachlan?!"

Murdoch's shoulders slumped as the golden faerie opened the drawing room door and stood, breathless and dishevelled, before them. "What do you want, fox?" he scowled, turning from Lachlan to rearrange the blankets on Sorcha's lap as he did so. "Surely nothing is so important it could not wait until morning."

A pause. And then: "I want to raise the baby."

Murdoch whipped back around to face Lachlan so quickly he almost lost his balance. "You *what?*" he exclaimed, releasing his hold on Sorcha's hand in order to storm over to the Seelie king. Murdoch was taller than him; he was gratified when Lachlan had to tilt his chin up slightly to meet his gaze.

The faerie's golden eyes narrowed. "I did not come

here to talk to you, horse. I am here to talk to Clara about being the babe's father."

"Too late, useless vermin," Murdoch grinned, glee washing over him as he realised Lachlan was going to get thoroughly rejected. He even took a few steps back to allow the faerie to approach Sorcha, get down on his knees and hold both her hands in his own, so sure in her answer as he was.

"Clara," Lachlan began, an eager smile on his face that implied he'd thoroughly ignored what Murdoch had just said. "Clara. *My* Clara. The wolf said that you would regain your mortality on the day your child was ready to sit upon a throne, but he did not specify which throne that must be. So let us raise this baby together, and prime him for *my* throne. I will happily give it up so that you can return to the life you wanted as fast as possible."

Sorcha's eyes widened in surprise; so did Murdoch's. *Lachlan has a point,* Murdoch thought, though it irked him to admit it. "That does not mean you have to be the baby's father," he told the faerie, who threw him a dismissive glance before returning his attention to Sorcha.

"But I *want* to," Lachlan said, squeezing Sorcha's hands as he did so. The same unreadable expression she had worn earlier had returned, which unnerved Murdoch to no end. Lachlan continued: "Clara, I have been thinking about this ever since we got you back from Eirian. We lost our child because of him. Let us raise this one together, instead."

Oh.

Murdoch's heart twisted at Lachlan's words. They were full of a raw, painful grief that the Seelie king had revealed to Murdoch only once before, immediately after he first learned of the loss of his child. It was impossible for Murdoch not to feel for him. *He has more claim than I to this child. But I cannot...*

He shook his head. Murdoch wanted to raise Sorcha's baby with her more than anything. And then:

"Both."

Murdoch blinked, turning his gaze to Sorcha's determined face in utter confusion. "What do you mean, both?"

"I mean that you can *both* be a father to my baby," she said, a flash of amusement lighting her eyes when Lachlan pulled away from her hands with an outraged yowl.

"You cannot be serious, Clara!" the faerie complained. He pointed at Murdoch. "You wish me and him to - to—"

"Sorcha, are you sure this is wise?" Murdoch cut in. He waved a hand uselessly in front of him. "To raise a child in such a way..."

"And how else would you suggest I raise my half-Unseelie, half-human baby, who needs to be protected from their sire's own people, prepped for the Seelie crown *and* be able to live some semblance of a happy life all at once?" Sorcha darted her eyes from Murdoch to Lachlan then back again. "I need you both in my life. I *want* you both in my life - for me and..."

When Sorcha lowered her gaze to her belly and ran a hand across it Murdoch softened immediately. "We will surely be no ordinary family," he murmured, reaching out to place a gentle hand over hers, "but if this is what you truly desire, Sorcha, then I am only too happy to oblige."

Sorcha beamed at him, the smile lighting up her face as if it was on fire. When she turned her head to look at Lachlan, Murdoch followed her gaze. The faerie stood there, watching them, a conflicted expression twisting his brow. But when Sorcha held out her other hand for him Lachlan immediately took it, and squeezed her fingers as if his life depended on it.

He threw a molten glare at Murdoch. "I won't be bested by a water horse. Just see, kelpie, I shall leave you in the dust. No father will be as great as I w—"

"Lachlan!" Sorcha scolded, though she was giggling. "I thought the two of you had finally reached some kind of understanding after all these years."

Murdoch snorted. "It would take a hundred years and more for things to change between us, my love."

"Well it's a good thing we have such a span of years," she replied, momentarily sober and serious.

When Lachlan reached forward and kissed her brow Murdoch did not stop him; he was impressed that he didn't even flinch at the display of affection. "We will do everything we can to raise the child good and true, Clara. And then..." He threw half a glance at Murdoch, who smiled.

"And then we can have the mortal life we want together," Murdoch finished. He smoothed Sorcha's wild hair away from her face, tucking an errant strand behind her ear as he did so. Her skin grew hot against his touch, and the way she traced her fingertips across his hand told Murdoch that they would perhaps not fall asleep quite as quickly as he had originally imagined they would once Lachlan left the Darrow house.

Sorcha let out a somewhat shaky sigh, then pulled

away from both Murdoch and Lachlan with a smile. Her eyes flicked to the bay window, though the curtains were drawn. It did not take Murdoch long to work out what she was thinking of, though it was Lachlan who spoke first.

"He will never touch you again," he swore. "You or the baby. If there is one thing the kelpie and I can agree on, it's that. And we have Beira on our side, who I must admit terrifies me."

Murdoch nodded. "The fox speaks the truth."

"As if I can speak anything but."

"Oh, but can you say each others' names?" Sorcha teased, a wicked smile painted on her lips.

The kelpie of Loch Lomond and the King of the Seelie Court looked at each other. Murdoch could see his reflection in Lachlan's eyes: dark-haired, broad-shouldered and pale-skinned. A stark difference from the faerie himself, with his bronzed hair, golden skin and narrow frame. They were opposites of each other down to their very cores. But one vital thing they shared, and it was the most important thing of all.

They both loved Sorcha Margaret Darrow.

"No," they said in unison, chuckling when Sorcha rolled her eyes and collapsed into her armchair in exaggerated exasperation.

"It is not my fault if my child grows up calling you both *fox* and *horse* instead of father," she warned.

Lachlan grinned. "Then we shall have to offer a trade to the bairn for the right ones: a name for a name. It is the faerie way, after all."

Murdoch resisted the urge to argue with Lachlan. For

the child *would* be a faerie, whether he liked it or not. It was up to himself and Sorcha to ensure the boy grew up to be a good one.

And, at the end of the day, not all faerie customs were bad ones.

Murdoch gave Lachlan the barest of smiles. "A name for a name."

EPILØGUE

Eirian

Sorcha Darrow's baby was born on the day of the summer solstice.

By the time news of the child's birth reached the ears of the Unseelie Court the sun had already dipped as low on the horizon as it would go that evening. So, in the everlasting twilight of midsummer at midnight, Eirian took on the guise of a raven to circle the realm of the Seelie. For he knew Sorcha would not be in the Darrow household – not when she needed to ensure the safety of her baby's birth.

His baby. Eirian's child and heir.

Even as a raven Eirian found it difficult to trick his way past the charms and spells Lachlan had woven over the Seelie Court. Bitterly he conceded that the young faerie truly was more powerful than he'd given him credit for, and would only grow more so with every passing day sitting on his throne as the golden king.

Eirian had been foolish to assume Evanna's son – despite being barely more than a boy in terms of years – would be green and inexperienced. He had brought Beira to his side, after all. Beira, whom even Eirian was wary of.

Lachlan was crafty. He was sneaky. He found solutions to problems where there should have been none.

He was a damn fox.

Eirian allowed air to fill his wings like sails, slowing his lazy, spiralling flight to a near-halt in order to survey the Seelie Court below him. All around him were trees and bushes laden with colourful faerie fruit, filling Eirian's nostrils with their heady, dangerous scent. Bright torches of orange and blue and flickering green flames lit the gemstone-encrusted path that led to the golden palace, which glittered even in the blanket of night. It was a beautiful place, the Seelie Court; Eirian had always appreciated its splendour.

"Where are you, my lovely queen?" he murmured, voice silky upon the warm nighttime breeze despite coming out of the beak of a raven. Eirian liked to think of Sorcha in such terms despite the fact he had made the fatal mistake of *not* marrying her whilst he had the opportunity to. But Eirian had taken Sorcha from Lachlan and the kelpie as a means to control them; marrying a human had never been something the Unseelie king would have considered doing.

But that was before. Before Sorcha became the mother of his one and only child – a rarity amongst his kind. Eirian was closing in on nine hundred years old, during which time not one of the babes he had put inside of faeries and mortals alike had survived past the first few months of pregnancy. That Sorcha had made it through childbirth with both her and the baby alive and well made her endlessly valuable in ways the girl likely could not yet fathom.

Once Eirian got his hands on Sorcha he would not make the same mistake again; whether through enchantment or blackmail he *would* make her his bride. That doing so would forever torment Lachlan and the water horse was a delicious bonus.

Off in the distance a fiddle was playing, and the sounds of laughter and dancing could be heard. *Celebrating my child's birth,* Eirian thought as he descended towards the ground. It was a good sign, for if most everyone in the Court was outside celebrating then there would be few creatures currently residing in the palace.

A lone faun on spindly legs glanced at Eirian as he flew past it to settle on the low boughs of an ash tree, close to an open window of the Seelie palace. He cawed at the animal, peeved that it did not immediately run away, before ignoring it in favour of peering inside the palace.

The window he'd stopped by looked in on the king's chambers; Eirian was pleased that his memory of the labyrinthine Seelie palace remained pinpoint accurate. Despite the heat of the evening a fire was roaring merrily in the intricately carved hearth, filling the room with the pleasant smell of woodsmoke. The flames were the main source of light, casting long, dark shadows into the far corners of the room.

Lachlan himself was nowhere to be seen, but the dark-haired human form of the kelpie was sitting cross-legged on the floor with his back against the bed. A painfully fond smile was painted across his face. In front of him, lying upon a pile of silken cushions and thick, woven blankets was a woman with wild, tangled hair, pale skin and rosy cheeks, clutching a bundle to her breast with the utmost care.

Sorcha and the babe.

"You are sure about the name?" the kelpie – Murdoch – asked, so softly that Eirian had to risk clambering over from the ash tree to sit upon the windowsill to hear him. "Lachlan might protest to it being far too...human."

Sorcha let out a gentle snicker, bending her head low to plant a kiss upon the baby. Eirian turned this way and that to try and catch a glimpse of the child from his vantage point but to no avail, which frustrated him beyond belief.

Move an inch to the left, he thought, willing Sorcha to do as he wished. *An inch, for just one look.*

"If Lachlan is concerned about the human nature of my *half-human* child then he can take it up with me," Sorcha told Murdoch, an exhausted but amused expression upon her face as she spoke.

It was his turn to laugh. "Take it up with you and lose, you mean."

"Exactly." She kissed the baby again. "If the name was good enough for my father then it's good enough for my son."

Eirian stilled. *A son. I have a son. Sorcha has given me everything centuries of women could not. But what was her father's name?*

Murdoch shuffled closer to Sorcha, sliding an arm around her waist to pull her against his side. She eagerly leaned her head against his shoulder. "I like William," he said. "It's a good name. Most of the *Williams* I ate over the years were honest, decent men."

"What a horrific thing to say!" Sorcha gasped, appalled, but then she giggled. "I suppose he'll have to get used to you saying such things, though. Do you think a half-human, half-Unseelie child has ever been raised by a kelpie father? *And* a Seelie father? The King of the Seelie Court, no less."

"I'm inclined to believe that the definitive answer to that is *no*," Murdoch replied. He kissed the crown of Sorcha's head and smoothed her hair back. "How are you feeling? I can hold little Will so you can rest."

But Sorcha declined with a shake of her unruly hair. "I am happy just the way I am," she said. And then, after a moment of contemplation: "I don't suppose I could convince you to find me some wine, though? Given the fact I gave birth just this afternoon I'd say I deserve it."

Murdoch chuckled as he stood up, giving Sorcha a half-mocking bow. "But of course. Your wish is my command, as it were."

Eirian watched as the man who was not a man left Lachlan's chambers. For a minute or two he did nothing but watch and feel and listen from his spot on the windowsill; Eirian could sense no faeries nearby, nor any other creature of consequence. It was just him in the form of a raven, Sorcha...and the baby.

With a final glance behind him Eirian took a risk and flew into Lachlan's chambers on silent wings. He landed on top of a handsomely carved wardrobe out of Sorcha's line of sight, pleased to see that she had not noticed him.

William, she named him, Eirian thought, when he was finally granted a view of the son she had given him. *It is not a bad name as far as human names go.*

He was every inch as beautiful as Eirian could have hoped. William's skin was a fainter silver-blue than a full Unseelie faeric; it shimmered and caught the flickering light of the fire in the most breathtaking of ways. His hair was just as starkly silver as his father's, but it had a slight curl to it that suggested the baby had inherited the same wildness of his mother's hair.

Eirian would have to wait and see if William's teeth and nails grew sharp like the Unseelie or rounded like a human's, though he did not care for such things right now. No, all he wanted was a glimpse of the boy's eyes.

Sorcha shifted William in her arms, cooing down at him as he gurgled back with eyes held tightly shut. Though she was clearly exhausted – barely five minutes away from falling into unconsciousness, Eirian reckoned – her expression grew bright when she gazed at her son. "Will you be a singer too, my love?" she asked him, gently touching the end of Will's nose with her index finger. "Would you like to sing with me now? I have a song for you."

Eirian cocked his feathered head to one side, wishing he had his own ears with which to listen as Sorcha began singing. She had thus far avoided granting him a song, after all, and though this one was not strictly for him it *was* for his son. Eirian would take it, and gladly.

"*Oh can ye sew cushions,*" Sorcha began, tickling William under his chin as she did so. "Your father – well, the kelpie one – loves this song. I hope you will love it too, little Will. *O can ye sew cushions,*"

"*And can ye sew sheets,*

And can ye sing ballalloo when the bairn greets?

And hee and haw birdie,

And hee and haw lamb,

And hee and haw, birdie, my bonnie wee lamb.

And hush a baw baby and balilly-loo,

And hee and haw birdie my bonnie wee doo."

Even though Eirian hated that the song belonged to the kelpie, he was enraptured. Sorcha's voice was lilting and lovely; he could listen to it for forever. *Would* listen to it for forever, when he found a way to lure Sorcha back to the Unseelie Court.

The lullaby should have sent William to sleep. Instead, the child slowly blinked open his eyes to stare at his mother as he continued to babble incoherently. And so it was that Eirian finally saw what colour they were: one green and one blue, like gems cut from the land and sea themselves.

His mother's eyes, he thought, swiftly flying out of the room when he sensed someone walking down the corridor towards the door. He did not want to leave – wanted to stay and watch his son grow from this very moment onward – but Eirian knew better than to risk being caught in such a place. He had seen what he needed to see, and had to be satisfied with that.

His mother's eyes, Eirian thought again, ascending into the starlit sky in ever-widening circles. He was pleased with that. More than pleased. Little Will would look like both of his parents, as was only right and proper. It would tie Sorcha to Eirian and his kingdom whether she wanted it or not.

William Darrow was perfect. All Eirian had to do was

wait a little longer to claim the boy and his mother as his own. It was something the Unseelie king could do, and do well; he'd practised patience for close to a millennium, after all.

Eirian had always played the long game, and now the end was finally in sight.

THE STORY WILL CONTINUE...

Just how long will it take for Will Darrow to ascend a faerie throne and grant his mother her longed-for mortality? Find out in the Dark Spear duology...soon.

If you love Uprooted, Howl's Moving Castle, and Shadow & Bone, then H. L. Macfarlane's enchanting mythology-soaked romantic fantasy, *Intended,* is for you! Read on for an excerpt.

A long silence stretched out, then, save for the twittering of a handful of morning birds which remained in Mt. Duega for the winter. Charlie tuned into the sound, breathing in the crisp air in an effort to reassure herself that she was not all that far from home – not really. She was still surrounded by her beloved woods. It *sounded* like her woods. It *smelled* like her woods.

Daniel Silver was staring straight at her.

Charlie flinched, then hated herself for doing so. The last thing she needed was for the man to think she was intimidated by him, though in truth she was. So when he beckoned with a finger for her to come closer Charlie bit back her nerves and walked towards him.

I feel like he's trying to work me out in one fell swoop, she mused, when Silver's gaze swept from her feet to her head, back down again, then settled on her eyes. For a moment Charlie genuinely believed that he *could* get her measure so quickly, and pushed out her Influence on instinct in order to direct him elsewhere.

But before the tendril of magic could reach Silver, Charlie coiled it back in. Her father would hate it if she Influenced her new employer – and she agreed with him. *It will only make my life harder,* she concluded. *I'd have to keep my magic active at all times to stop him from realising someone is working it upon him in the first place.*

For Charlie had no doubts left in her mind about just how powerful Daniel Silver was now that she was finally in close proximity to him. Her father hadn't lied; the raw magic emanating off him was staggering. The urge to Influence him returned, just for a moment, when Charlie's curiosity over how much of her own magic she'd have to use to break through Silver's defences overwhelmed her.

Once more Charlie had to reign herself in. *Focus on something else. Like his glasses. They're definitely prescription,* she thought, tilting her head to see the slight distortion the lenses caused to Silver's face.

"Just what is it that you're thinking, Miss Hope?" the man asked, noting where Charlie's attention was with passive interest.

"That a magician as strong as you shouldn't be wearing glasses."

"Coming from a young woman who didn't deem it necessary to brush her hair nor tuck in her shirt for her first day at a new job?"

Both quips left their respective tongues in close succession of each other, leaving Charlie in no doubt what the man's first impression of her was. *So he's obsessed with image,* she concluded, glancing down to see that her shirt was indeed untucked. She made no attempt to fix it nor to tidy her hair, which was always unkempt when Charlie left it unbound.

Her decision not to tidy herself up was clearly noted by Silver. His nose wrinkled in distaste, causing his glasses to slide downwards. When he pushed then back up Charlie couldn't help but say, "That wouldn't happen if you fixed your eyesight."

"My personal preferences aren't of your concern. Are you always this rude upon meeting people for the first time?"

"Rude?" Charlie blinked her eyes innocently. "I'm merely making an observation."

"Yes, with the intent of being rude."

Oh, you have no idea, she thought, resisting the urge to say something else that would most definitely be construed as such. Instead, Charlie crossed her arms over her chest and attempted to stare down her new employer. When he remained silent she asked, "So where am I staying, anyway? Or are we going to stand out here all day?"

In lieu of answering her question Silver took a step towards her and mirrored Charlie's crossed arms.

Another frown furrowed his brow, causing his glasses to slip once more.

Behind the lenses Charlie noted his eyes were very, very blue.

"Are you a Mind or Matter magician?" Silver demanded, clearly discomfited by the fact he hadn't been able to work it out yet.

Charlie resisted the urge to smile at this invisible victory, then replied honestly, "I'm useless with Matter."

"Mind, then. Any specific strengths?"

"I don't know. I guess you'll have to find out for your —"

"Miss Hope, I'm warning you. I don't have the patience to deal with this attitude of yours."

"I guess you'll have to fire me, then."

For the briefest of moments Charlie was certain that Silver was about to explode. His temple twitched, and his hands gripped his forearms with tense, barely-constrained irritation. She prepared herself for a shout. A curse. An immediate dismissal.

Instead Silver closed his eyes, exhaled, then turned back towards his expansive house. "Uthesh give me strength, I understand exactly what you're doing. Follow me, Miss Hope."

Well that didn't work out the way I wanted it to, Charlie sulked, nonetheless dutifully following Mr Silver into his abode. *I suppose Da would never forgive me if I deliberately got myself fired.*

The man strode far too quickly through his house for Charlie to make out much of her surroundings, but since the morning sunlight hadn't reached the corridors yet she knew it was pointless to try and memorise the layout, anyway. When a tawny cat leapt from a shadowy windowsill into Silver's arms moments later Charlie jumped in fright.

But then Mr Silver smiled, and all she could focus on was him.

Gone was his detached demeanour and barely-contained temper. Faint lines creased the sides of his eyes, which lit up at the mere sight of the animal. He looked happy. Normal.

Like a mortal human being, not a man who was going to live forever.

"Kit," Silver said to the cat, scratching its chin before bopping its forehead with his own. "Just where have you been hiding all these weeks?"

The cat – Kit – mewed in response before turning its impossibly green eyes on Charlie. She took a small step back in shock.

It's from the woods. Daniel Silver is friends with an animal kin of the Immortal Folk?

Charlie supposed she shouldn't be surprised. Silver's estate was right on the boundary of Duega woods and he was immortal himself. It *shouldn't* have been a surprise.

Except that it was.

Never in all her twenty-four years had Charlie known another soul who fraternised with creatures from the woods.

When Kit meowed at her Charlie was brought starkly back into the present. Silver was staring at her staring at his cat, who jumped from his arms to slink down the corridor. Charlie turned her head to watch Kit leave until he disappeared around a corner.

"Miss Hope."

"Yes?" she murmured, attention still on the tawny forest cat.

"In here," Silver said, opening a door on his left and indicating inside when Charlie finally focused on him once more. All signs of his previous easy smile were gone.

Numbly Charlie entered the room, careful to give Mr Silver a wide berth as she did so. Her Influence magic was exacerbated by close contact; for years now she had barely touched another soul, save her father.

Inside the room was sparsely furnished with high-quality, oak-carved pieces: a high-backed bed, a wardrobe, a chest of drawers, a desk, a full-length mirror and a chair.

"My Chief-of-Staff will deal with you shortly," Silver said when Charlie perched upon the bed, testing the spring of the mattress with splayed fingers. "Don't treat her with the same disrespect you have thus far shown me."

Charlie clucked her tongue, keeping her eyes averted as she muttered, "I wouldn't dream of it."

The shudder of the door not-quite-slamming closed was all the reply Charlie got. But when she strained her ears she just barely heard Silver lament, "Just what have I agreed to?"

She threw herself onto her back with a smile. Silver may have worked out that she was trying to get fired but that didn't mean he *wouldn't* fire her.

After all, if Charlie was the most incompetent

employee Daniel Silver had ever taken on then he'd have no choice but to dismiss her...or risk the wrath of his political sponsors who had all so desperately wished to have their children taken under the man's wing.

A small, mischievous laugh left Charlie's lips. "I give him a week."

ACKNÖWLEDGEMENTS

King of Forever concludes the Bright Spear trilogy, but as you've seen from the way it ends this is not the conclusion of the story for Sorcha, Lachlan, Murdoch and Eirian. No, it is merely an appropriate pause before the second half of the story is explored in the Dark Spear duology!

I have loved every minute spent working on King of Forever and its predecessors, even when I was in the midst of procrastinating (which was often). Writing my own Scottish fairy tale was a dream come true; nine-year-old me would be very proud.

So which team are you all on? Team Lachlan? Team Murdoch? Or, shock horror, team *Eirian*? The obvious point by the end of King of Forever was that Sorcha did not really have to choose between her fox and her kelpie, because their love for her – and her love for them – was too strong to be constrained by typically human notions of monogamy. Also, they're supernatural creatures. If they want to have a twisted polyamorous thing going on then I say we let them. It's definitely working for Ailith, after all.

I am very excited to bring William Darrow to life. I think you'll either love him or hate him, which is always a good thing.

As usual I would like to thank my partner, Jake; our

lovely bunnies; my best friend and editor, Kirsty and, of course, my fans. The reaction to the Bright Spear trilogy has been huge, and I am truly amazed and grateful for it.

Until the next one!

Hayley

ABOUT THE AUTHOR

Hayley Louise Macfarlane hails from the very tiny hamlet of Balmaha on the shores of Loch Lomond in Scotland. After graduating with a PhD in molecular genetics she did a complete 180 and moved into writing fiction. Though she loves writing multiple genres (fantasy, romance, sci-fi, psychological fiction and horror so far!) she is most widely known for her Gothic, Scottish fairy tale, Prince of Foxes – book one of the Bright Spear trilogy.

You can follow her on Twitter at @HLMacfarlane.

ORIGIN OF POEMS

Underground (David Bowie; 1986)
Ae Fond Kiss (Robert Burns; 1791)
Home (Robert Burns; 1786)
Ca' the Yowes (Robert Burns; 1794)
O Can Ye Sew Cushions (Robert Burns; 1787)

ALSO BY H. L. MACFARLANE

FAIRY TALE SHARED UNIVERSE:
BRIGHT SPEAR TRILOGY
PRINCE OF FOXES
LORD OF HORSES
KING OF FOREVER

DARK SPEAR DUOLOGY
SON OF SILVER (COMING 2023)
HEIR OF GOLD (COMING 2023)

ALL I WANT FOR CHRISTMAS IS A FAERIE ASSASSIN?!

CHRONICLES OF CURSES
BIG, BAD MISTER WOLFE
SNOWSTORM KING
THE TOWER WITHOUT A DOOR

OTHER BOOKS:
GOLD AND SILVER DUOLOGY
INTENDED
REVIVAL (RELEASE DATE TBC)

MONSTERS TRILOGY
INVISIBLE MONSTERS
INSATIABLE MONSTERS (COMING OCTOBER 2022)
INVINCIBLE MONSTERS (COMING 2023)

THRILLERS
THE BOY FROM THE SEA

ROM-COMS
THE UNBALANCED EQUATION
COURTNEY CAN'T DECIDE (RELEASE DATE TBC)

SHORT STORIES
THE SNOWDROP (PART OF ONCE UPON A WINTER: A FOLK
AND FAIRY TALE ANTHOLOGY)
THE GOAT
THE BOY WHO DID NOT FIT